HER RETREAT

ITALIAN LOVERS (BOOK 2)

DIANA FRASER

BAY BOOKS

Her Retreat
(Also published as *Seduced by the Italian*)
by Diana Fraser

© 2012 Diana Fraser

—Italian Lovers Series—

The Italian's Perfect Lover
Seduced by the Italian
The Passionate Italian
An Accidental Christmas

For more information about this author visit: dianafraser.com of you can
sign up to Diana's newsletter here.

CHAPTER 1

*H*e was late.

Isabella, Contessa Di Sorano, fixed her gaze on the coffin as it was lowered into the waiting grave, all the while acutely aware of the man who'd arrived only minutes earlier and now stood beside her.

Not just late, but too late.

She focused on her breathing, determined to control the anger that simmered inside her, as hot as the Tuscan sun. Why had he come now, when his grandmother was dead, when he was no longer wanted?

From beneath her broad-brimmed black hat and sunglasses she could see only his immaculately pressed black trousers and highly polished shoes that reflected back the harsh sunlight as if it had no effect on him, as if nothing could touch him.

She turned her gaze back to the coffin. Once, everything had touched him but it seemed he'd hardened over the years. She wondered briefly if his eyes—which had always been so warm and passionate—reflected the change, but she refused to shift, to look at him, to acknowledge him.

Heat enveloped her, making it hard to breathe. She felt trapped by her sleek black dress and the stiletto shoes that were as unyielding as the sun-hardened soil upon which she stood.

Sadness and anger formed a lump in her throat and a throbbing in her head that surged and retreated like the pulsing rhythm of the cicadas. She tightened her grip around the flowers she'd picked that morning, trying to distract her mind by pressing their woody, rough stems into the palms of her hands. It didn't work.

She'd wondered how she'd feel when he returned. And now she knew—exactly the same. It was as if the seven years hadn't passed. But there was one difference. She'd learned how to hide her feelings.

She closed her eyes so she could see nothing of him. But the tiniest shift of air brought a thread of his expensive after-shave drifting across to her. Her nostrils flared in response, her heart quickened and she swallowed. He'd never worn that before. It would have been too expensive. But now, apparently nothing was too expensive, too out of his reach, apart from spending the last few days with his grandmother.

She drew in another deep breath of air—a complex mix of his aftershave, wild oregano and the scent of the disturbed earth—and glanced at the priest who had fallen silent.

He nodded and she stepped forward and scattered a bunch of white wildflowers—beloved by her old nurse for their tenacity—on top of the casket. She looked down as if the coffin lid were not there; as if the lined and resigned face with the all-seeing eyes looked straight back up at her. Her breath caught in her throat and she gasped and stepped back abruptly, stumbling on the uneven ground.

A hand reached around her to steady her. She closed her eyes against the power of the fingers that pressed into her waist, against their warmth on her already heated body, and against the slide of his fingers across her back as he withdrew his hand, as if aware his support wasn't wanted.

She didn't turn around; she didn't acknowledge his touch, simply stood looking down at the grave, trying to hold back the tide of feeling that surged inside her.

Dust hung in the air as people filed by and dropped handfuls of soil onto the coffin before walking away. When it was her turn she scooped up a handful of the dry lumpy earth that looked too hard, too rough, to drop onto her old friend. She rubbed it between her fingers, the soil working under her manicured nails, until it grew soft. Only then did she let it rain gently onto the coffin.

It was time to move on. The old lady would have understood. She'd have insisted. Isabella stepped back, hesitating for one last look at the flowers that were already bruised and wilting and then turned and walked to where her friends stood.

She felt his eyes on her. She knew only he remained behind. Let him. She had nothing to say to him.

ISABELLA SIGHED, kicked off her shoes and curled up on the window seat of the western tower of the Castello Romitorio. It had been a long day. The party continued downstairs but she couldn't face it—nor him. Here, in this empty room, she was safe. For today, at least, because tomorrow it would be her home no longer. She closed her eyes and let her mind drift.

It was the draft of cooler evening air that first alerted her to his presence. A chill wave of alarm swept through her body as she snapped open her eyes to see the figure of a man standing in front of one of the large stone-framed windows. The saffron rays of the evening sun shone directly behind him, lighting up the motes of dust he'd disturbed and illuminating only his silhouette: shadowed face turned toward her, broad shoulders, elbows jutting as he thrust his hands into his trouser pockets.

"What the hell are you doing here?" Her voice was hoarse as if forced through a filter of raw emotion.

"I've come to see you." His voice was deeper than she remembered.

With his face partly in shadow, she couldn't see his expression. She didn't *want* to see his expression. Awkwardly she looked down and then away, out of the window, anywhere but at him. "Well, you've seen me. Now perhaps you'll leave."

He walked up to her and she felt his presence encroaching on her space as much as his physical body. Both were more than she could deal with.

He stopped immediately behind her. "Are you ever going to look at me?"

"And why would I want to do that?"

"It's usual."

She turned slightly toward him, her head still lowered, unwilling to reveal anything to this man who had once meant so much to her; the man who had been instrumental in bringing disaster to her and her family.

"It's usual to be on time for your grandmother's funeral. It's usual to be with the woman who'd raised you when she's dying. It's usual to have kept in contact with her over the years. I think you have no sense of what is, and what isn't, usual."

She twisted in her seat and slipped her shoes back on her feet. Her hand trembled as she smoothed her already smooth hair, checking its length was intact in the perfect, low knot.

"Cara, I've long since come to believe that nothing is usual. Least of all my life, least of all yours."

His voice had softened, had become a caress that melted something she'd frozen long ago. She looked up at him then and what she saw wasn't what she'd expected to see.

While his clothes were immaculate, he looked tired and disheveled. Stubble darkened his chin, his black hair was too long and fell away from his face in rough waves and his honey-brown eyes were underscored by dark shadows. But it was his eyes that drew her. They hadn't hardened like she'd anticipated but still held the same passion and fire she remembered, except now the heat was tempered with a maturity and sadness she'd never seen before.

She barely saw the boy she'd once known in this man; he was broader, more powerful than she remembered. But she *felt* he was the same: it was the same feeling his eyes gave her when she looked into them; it was the same sensation of wanting to close the gap between them, that his body gave. Her eyes stung with heat and pain.

She saw from his reaction he'd registered her unwanted emotions. His frown lifted and the brown of his eyes darkened with the unmistakable flare of desire. He pulled his hands from his pockets and started forward, as if to reach for her. She held up her hand to stop him and looked away, shifting back against the window. She had to stop this. She needed to protect herself. She took a deep breath and faced him again, prepared this time for the onslaught of emotional turmoil that just seeing him, feeling him close, brought to her.

"You're wrong, Luca. Come on, tell me, why are you here? You failed to be with your grandmother during her last days and almost missed her funeral."

"I had no choice." His voice was quiet, contained by a tension in the tight lines around his mouth.

"Right. Something else came up more important than your grandmother. Business, no doubt. You've become your father, just as my father predicted. Business above all else. Why bother to come at all?"

His eyes narrowed dangerously—just as they used to whenever he spoke of the father who'd deserted him—and his jaw clenched as he worked at controlling the anger her words had evoked. But it was a relief to see some emotion other than the heat of desire in his eyes.

"As I said, something else came up. My grandmother knew about it."

"Your grandmother knew? Come on, you haven't seen her in years."

"I kept in contact."

"She didn't say anything."

"Perhaps she didn't tell you everything. Why should she tell you about my calls, my visits? You'd made it clear you felt nothing for me, wanted nothing further to do with me."

She had. But, despite that, she felt a flicker of betrayal at her old friend keeping this from her; allowing her to think that Luca hadn't cared enough to see her.

"Of course. It's none of my business anyway. But it still doesn't explain why you're here, now."

"To see you; to talk with you."

"There's nothing to talk about."

He exhaled roughly and walked away, his quick gaze scanning the room. "I knew you'd be here. I watched you at the funeral and knew you'd come."

A knot tightened in her chest. "It's just somewhere to catch my breath."

"No, it's more than that. It was always your retreat, the place you came to find yourself. And, of course, it was the place we found each other."

"You think I've come here because of you?"

His eyes flickered over her face, his expression thought-ful. "Why not? Re-live the moments we shared here together." He looked around. "But back then it was not so sparsely furnished. What happened to the old sofa?"

She swallowed hard and tried to still the hammering of her heart as the memories came flooding back to her: of the first time he slowly undid the buttons of her dress and of the brush of his finger against her skin; of the way his hair—always too long—had tickled her breasts as his lips explored her body; of the way they'd fallen in a tangle of limbs onto the old sofa, and of the feel of him inside her.

She stood up and opened the window, closing her eyes against the cooling evening breeze, trying without success to dispel the heat her thoughts had created.

"The sofa's gone. I had to clear everything out. You know, of course, the castello was sold a year ago?"

"Si."

"And that the year's grace the owner gave us to settle our affairs has now expired?"

"You did what you had to do to pay off your father's debts. You can make a new start for you and your sisters. You can return to England where you spent so much time with your mother's family."

"I may sound English, but I *feel* Italian. Five hundred years, Luca, half a millennium the castello has been in my family and now it's gone. I've had to let it go."

He shrugged. "Traditions are made to be broken."

She shook her head. "You'll never understand."

"No, why would I? I have no traditions, no background, as your father made clear to me." Isabella opened her mouth to speak. "You've no need to defend him." Luca shrugged. "He was right." He sighed and looked around the empty room. "But now it's all gone anyway." He swept his hand the length of the empty bookshelves that lined one of the walls between two of the four windows. "And the books have gone, too. But the shelves remain. I built them well."

The silence was filled with the memories of seven years before when Luca had worked on small building jobs around the castello and had built the shelves.

"You were always good at your work."

His hand sought out the carving on the side of the shelves. "Still here."

"You etched it in with your pen-knife: a deeply-cut heart never fades away, no matter how much work one does to eradicate the damage."

His hand instantly stopped moving and he frowned, turning slowly toward her again. "Depends on how deep the damage went. I can erase it if you'd like me to."

"Please do. The castle isn't mine any more. The new owner is to take vacant possession tomorrow and so I'm sure he, or she, would appreciate any graffiti removed."

"Graffiti," he murmured. "Yes, I'll organize it for you."

"Not for me. For the new owner. Now, if you'll excuse me I have a meeting to attend." She began to move away but he placed a hand lightly on her arm and she stopped dead in her tracks.

"Isabella, tell me, did she suffer?"

For the first time since he'd entered the room she looked, really looked, into his eyes and saw a raw pain that cut through everything else.

She balled her hands tightly to stop them from reaching out to him and shook her head. "No, Luca, she didn't. We made sure of that." She blinked to hold back the tears that threatened. "I'm sorry. I'm so sorry."

"You were with her when she died?"

Isabella nodded.

"Good. She loved you."

Isabella gasped sharply as grief threatened to overwhelm her. "And I, her. She passed peacefully. She was just waiting to go."

"Si, si." He nodded, looking down at the ancient floor-boards, now bare of rugs. "My grandmother was a patient woman." He looked back at her again. "Unlike her grandson."

Isabella felt a smile tug at her lips.

"Yes. Unlike her grandson, who could never wait for anything."

"I waited for you."

The atmosphere changed in a heartbeat. As the sun slipped behind the mountain ridge, a dense twilight fell on them, as heavy as the shadows of the past that still haunted her.

"Not long enough, Luca."

"I gave you until the end of summer. How long did I have to wait until you agreed to see me? Three months, three years?"

"More than one month, more than a deadline by which time if I didn't see you, you'd be gone. More than that."

"No, face it, Isabella, after your father's death you let your family persuade you I wasn't good enough. No amount of waiting would have changed that. It was that simple."

"Nothing is that simple." She shook her head, with increasing impatience, increasing fear. She could scarcely control her trembling body.

"Then what was it? Tell me. I've a right to know. You wouldn't see me, wouldn't reply to my phone calls, my emails, my letters. Why?"

The words choked her throat; her mouth was unable to form the sounds that would make him understand. She pressed her hand to her chest to try to stop the quickened breathing that threatened to balloon into a full-blown panic attack. Painful memories unfurled and lashed out at her like a poisonous snake, always waiting to bite, always hungry.

"Because I couldn't think straight."

"Thinking wasn't required. If you'd had any feelings for me you'd have come to me. But you didn't."

She stepped away from him, needing to move, needing to ground herself in the reassurance of the familiar. But there were no lamps to turn on, nothing but emptiness.

"Don't do this, Luca, not now."

"While I might be impatient, you were never good at facing things, were you Isabella? You always retreated, back into your family, back into yourself, where I could never reach you."

"Perhaps that means I don't wish to be reached."

"Perhaps." The space between them was bridged swiftly as he stepped forward and stood in front of her. He was so close that she couldn't see the whole of his face any more, just the parts: his brow drawn down as if puzzled; his eyes focusing on the individual elements of her face also, as if they were something he was only now remembering; and his lips, their tension suddenly softening.

As if in a dream he raised his hand to her hair and, so lightly she scarcely felt it, trailed the back of his finger down its sleek length. His eyes followed his finger's movement along her cheek and neck where he stopped, his fingers curling around her chin. He looked into her eyes with a depth of sadness that surprised her.

"Perhaps," he continued, "but I doubt it."

She wanted to push his hand away but was stilled by the flood of long-forgotten sensations that his touch loosed. Her gaze dropped to his mouth. She licked her lips as if her tongue wanted to explore the soft swell of his lower lip but had to be content with her own. She hoped he couldn't hear her quickened heart beat that filled her body with an urgent rhythm, compelling her to move closer to him.

"You always did think you knew me better than I knew myself."

His mouth quirked at the corners in an echo of the mischievous smile she'd known years before. "And I was right."

Before she could respond he'd dipped his head to hers and brushed her lips gently with his own. It was as if all the strength she'd spent years building had fled from her body and mind leaving only a clawing need. For an instant she shifted closer to him so their lips met once more but at the touch of his hands, running down the sides of her body, she was jolted back into awareness and pulled away.

She felt bereft—and humiliated. Within five minutes of being alone she'd made it plain that she was his for the taking. Had he come simply to do this? To show her up? To make a fool of her?

"Leave me be, Luca. I can't do this. I don't want this. You must go now. I have a meeting with my lawyer." She dragged her gaze away, walked to the door opened it and waited for him to walk through.

He looked down at the bare floor for a long moment, before he turned to her, his eyes cool now. "So you have no regrets then, Isabella?"

"Why would I have?"

"Because we loved each other once; because you turned me away because I wasn't good enough for you and your family; because you didn't tell me about our child until it was too late. No regrets for any of that?"

He didn't even sound bitter. Stated it as if he truly believed every single word.

She shook her head in confusion, unable to break through the barriers of guilt and grief and tell him the truth.

"None then. I see."

He didn't look at her as he walked out of the room. She heard his footfall on the spiral staircase, descending, moving away from her just as he had seven years before.

With one last glance around the beautiful room that had once witnessed the love affair that had changed her life, she closed the door.

THE SHARP CLICK of her heels on the stone-flagged floor echoed around the great hall, now stripped of its priceless carpets and hangings. Numbly she passed through pools of grey twilight that crept in through arched windows, punctuating the darkness with a light that made the dark more sinister.

Part of her wanted to run away—leave immediately and go far away from here—from the memories seeing Luca again had unleashed. But the same impulse that had made her work hard at her interior design practice these past seven years to keep her sisters; the same impulse that controlled every aspect of how she appeared, of how she behaved, kept her walking toward the library. She had no choice but to carry on—to complete the paperwork on the castello and her new contract—because she still had responsibilities to her remaining family. She owed them.

She hesitated briefly outside the reception room where she heard the wine-fueled chatter and laughter of people sharing anecdotes of the past and hopes for the future as they continued to grieve for the old lady. Luca would be there. No doubt charming the villagers he'd been raised amongst with stories of his new life, lived among riches that most of them couldn't even dream of. That was what he'd always wanted: a new life away from the old. And that's what he'd got. Abruptly she turned and continued onto the library. Even if she had time she couldn't risk seeing him again because she couldn't face the memories that his presence unraveled in her.

As the heavy oak door to the library swung open, Isabella's gaze was drawn to the lawyer, who sat to one side of the desk, his papers spread under the light of a lamp. He stood up as she entered and walked to greet her.

"Buona sera, Santino."

"Contessa."

She shook hands, increasingly puzzled by her lawyer's uncharacteristic frown. Then, as he moved back to his seat, she saw Luca. He sat in the other chair in front of the desk, one foot nonchalantly resting on the other knee. Even as her body prickled with alarm, she felt the chill of control slide into place. It was habitual now; it was her only defense.

"What are you doing here?"

"Same as you. Business."

She looked questioningly at the lawyer. He looked down, embarrassed, and nodded in agreement. "Signore Vittori is required to be here also."

"Is that so?" She was reassured by the cool, smooth tone of her voice.

"Si, Contessa. Please be seated and we will proceed." She hesitated but it was the lawyer's look of deep sympathy and understanding that made her move behind the desk and take her seat. Something had shifted, changed, without her knowing.

The lawyer cleared his throat and began to speak. Isabella looked down at the papers that the lawyer nudged from side to side with his pen. She tried to focus on the words of legal jargon that fell from his lips like so many darts onto an open wound. But they began merging into one as Isabella's mind refused to move beyond one name that kept recurring: Luca Vittori.

She held up her hand. "Please stop." She felt sick to her stomach with the knowledge that she couldn't yet accept. "Stop this. Just tell me in plain speech."

"Si, Contessa. As you are aware,"—again the solicitous

smile that made Isabella more fearful than anything else
—"you sold the castle a year ago but now the owner requires
vacant possession."

Isabella nodded, her neck and head stiff with anticipation.
"And as you are aware, Santino, the castle has been cleared of
all possessions still belonging to my family. Those remaining
have been purchased by the owner."

"Indeed. And you have signed the requisite documents
regarding the sale. And you have also agreed, informally, to
work with the owner on the castle's refurbishment."

It was a statement but the lawyer looked at her expec-
tantly. She nodded in agreement.

"Yes. For a period of three months. And I'm here to sign
the paperwork for that contract. But what this has to do with
Signore Vittori, I—"

"Isabella," Luca's voice was soft yet immediately she registered its impact and turned to him. "Don't you understand
yet? *I* am the owner. I bought the castle a year ago. It is me
who hired you for your services."

She knew; of course, she knew. The man who'd begun the
fracturing of her family and its subsequent decline in fortune
seven years before, the man who'd started all this, was now
finishing it.

"Why didn't you tell me?"

"I had my reasons."

"I'm sure you did. You always have a reason for everything, don't you? And I'm sure I know the reason. You
needed to take revenge on my family. The boy who had
nothing has now bought out the family who spurned him. It's
a reason. But it's a pretty pathetic reason."

The scrape of the lawyer's chair alerted her to his presence. "If you can sign here, contessa, signore, I will leave."

The harsh light of the lamp leached all the color and

contours from Luca's face. It was the face of a stranger, unreadable.

"You are mistaken, Isabella. I have no thirst for revenge. I assume you say this because you're upset." His voice was quiet and restrained.

"I say this because it is the only logical reason I can think of."

"Perhaps in your world of snobbery and retribution. But in mine?" He shook his head. "No. The disdain your family showed me never made me feel less of a man then, or now. I have no need to hit out, to seek revenge."

"Then why buy the castello?"

"I made a promise to someone."

"I don't believe you."

He shrugged. "It doesn't matter what you believe. Are you going to sign the contract or not? Santino is looking uncomfortable and wishes to leave."

A flushed smile from the lawyer confirmed Luca's observation. The truth was, she had no choice but to accept the contract. It would give her the money for her family to begin a new life. She leaned forward and signed her name.

Luca didn't move immediately, he simply watched her through narrowed eyes. Slowly a small smile settled on his lips and lit up his eyes with what she assumed to be satisfaction. He thought he'd won.

Anger pulsed through her veins, giving her the strength to fight back the memories his earlier tenderness had freed. Looking at him now—so sure of himself, so arrogant—the anger won and her memories receded like a low, spring tide, so distant they left no trace.

Her gaze rested easily on him now. Any lingering thought that he was there to see her—that he still felt something for her—had now vanished. He was out for revenge—whatever he might claim—and he'd achieved it. Knowing this she could face him and work for him. Her painful memories were in no danger of resurrection now.

Luca's smile faded and he leaned forward and signed his name with a flourish, taking up twice the space of her signature.

The lawyer blotted the signatures, shuffled the papers together and made a rapid exit, leaving a chill silence between them that no longer held possibility, only distance.

CHAPTER 2

*W*early Luca rose and walked over to the window. Lights from the village twinkled in the valley but all around them the dark mountains folded in on the castello. *Dio*, he needed a drink.

"May I?" He didn't have to see Isabella to feel her tight fury, controlled but no less present for all that. It ground into his fatigue even further. He may have missed his grandmother's funeral but her last request to him would haunt him for months to come.

"May you what?"

He sighed and turned to her then. Her grey gaze was direct and strong and cool and held no hint of the anger he felt from her.

"Pour myself a drink?" He gestured to the decanter and glasses on the cabinet. The library was obviously the last place to be packed away. Business. Of course, business over the personal any day.

Her cool gaze cracked as she glanced at the decanter, betraying some inward emotion which he had no chance to interpret as it was quickly replaced by the direct gaze once more. "If you must. As of now you own it anyway."

His mouth watered at the sight of the rich amber of the whisky: it seemed his only comfort of late. He tossed back a large mouthful and turned to her. "Would you like one?"

"No. What I want is for you to tell me exactly what you require of me. I wish to be clear."

He leaned against the window frame and studied her. How had such intimacy turned into such distance? He felt the chill in the atmosphere and he saw the chill in her pristine image. She had always been beautiful but now there was an edge that contained it. She looked closed. He pushed himself off the window and sighed. "Clarity is good." He walked back over to her and sat down. "Well, Isabella, I want the castello refurbished."

"That much, I'd gathered. Anyone could do that. Why me?"

"Because you know the place." It was true but certainly not the main reason he'd employed her. "And knowing the place, with your eye, you'll do a good job."

"And how am I to refurbish my home exactly? What is wrong with it?"

He smiled at her instant prickling. "You know perfectly well what's wrong with it. You've done your best with the family heirlooms but you've had no money to make it into the place you'd always envisaged it being."

A spark of interest momentarily warmed her cool eyes, sweeping away the shadows like sunshine between clouds. She'd used to talk of how the castello could be transformed with color and fabrics and cutting-edge designer furniture. Then the clouds lowered once more.

"So presumably you want a stylish home to which you can bring your wealthy friends." She stood up, her back ramrod straight, the smooth sweep of her brows framing her level gaze. "That's fine. I'll see you in the morning and show you some ideas."

He noticed she had no difficulty in looking at him now. But now it emphasized the distance between them. He used to be able to read her like a book, but not any more.

"You have it wrong. I have no wish for a show home."

"Come on," her laugh was hollow. "That's what you've bought the place for isn't it? To impress your friends and enemies, to thumb your nose at me? Why pretend otherwise?"

He ground his teeth, willing himself not to rise to the bait. He placed his whisky glass on the table with deliberate precision.

"Again, you are mistaking your petty feelings for my own. An easy mistake to make when one lives such a narrow life. However, you are entirely incorrect. I will not be living here. I want you to turn it into a family home."

He hadn't thought about the effect of his words until he saw the hurt cut through her eyes, like the fracturing of a glaze. She turned away swiftly. It was only then that he thought that perhaps she did regret aborting their baby. She shuffled the papers together that lay spread before her and dropped them into a folder.

"And why is that? Easier to sell?"

"*Certo*. I'm a property developer. That's what I do."

Her fine, dark brows rose and fell with derision. "I thought it was cities you developed: Sydney office towers, commercial buildings." She waved her hand dismissively.

Any sympathy at her hurt was swept away at her offhand referral to the business empire he'd created. "Money doesn't sound so bad when you need it though, does it, Isabella?"

She walked to the door. "I'll work on some plans and let you have them tomorrow."

No-one else got to him like Isabella did. Not even his ex

wife.

"Breakfast—at 7am. I want preliminary plans then."

"I'll have to work all night."

"Si. I'm paying you enough, I expect you to be available to me twenty-four hours a day."

"You haven't bought all my time. I still have a private life."

"No you don't. I've bought you for the next three months. It's *my* money that will fund the townhouse for you and your sisters; it's *my* money that will ensure your sisters' education. You owe me Isabella, and I suggest you begin to realize that."

He took another swig of whisky, angry with himself for letting slip one of the confidences his grandmother had told him.

"How do you know about the townhouse?"

"I make it my business to know."

"But this isn't business is it? It's personal. You *do* want to humiliate me. I just don't know why you pretend otherwise."

He shrugged. "You can think what you like."

"If I'm wrong, tell me."

He let the silence slip and lengthen between them. He'd promised his grandmother to look after Isabella. And he'd also promised her that he wouldn't tell her. His grandmother had known if Isabella knew the truth her pride would force her to turn away from the contract that would ensure her and her sisters' future.

"You can't, can you? You never ran from the truth before. You've changed so much."

"And you, too, Isabella."

"Then there's nothing further to say."

She closed the door behind her, leaving a silence redolent with anger and betrayal. But who had betrayed whom? Luca didn't know any more.

With his back to the window he finished his whisky and slid it along the table. But he didn't leave. Instead, he remembered. Seven years before, he'd been in the same room at Isabella's father's insistence.

The large man's handsome face had been almost purple with anger as he's spat out his disdain for Luca and his father, warning him to leave Isabella alone, warning him to get out of the village. He felt the anger surge again, just as it had done then, just as it had when he'd grabbed the older man by his collar and held him there in a tight grasp and watched fear flicker across his face. He could have inflicted serious damage on him, but he didn't. Instead he'd walked. Because part of him agreed with Isabella's father. Luca wasn't good enough; he had nothing to offer her.

He flicked off the lamp and listened to Isabella's footsteps retreat to the guest wing where she'd be staying.

"Well, Nonna," he looked up into the heavens, across the black valley, "I hope you're pleased. Because this is going to be much, much harder than I ever thought."

THE MORNING SUN streamed across the desk as Luca punched out short email replies. He'd been working since before dawn, trying to catch up on the backlog of work that his absence had created.

He continued to work as the door opened and footsteps advanced toward him. He didn't even look up when he heard Isabella clear her throat, merely indicated that she should sit. Aware that she was watching him, he let the minutes slide by as he finished his work, quietly closed the laptop and looked across the desk at her.

She was immaculately dressed, as usual, with her hair scraped back in a sleek French twist, gleaming pearls and a plain navy dress that fitted her like a glove and whose silk shimmered, iridescent, under the sun's early morning rays.

"You said you wanted to see me."

"Si. Do you have any ideas to show me?"

"Sure." She pushed across the papers and, as she bent low over them, he noticed dark smudges of shadow under her eyes and a slight tremor of her hand as she held the papers.

He leaned forward and pressed a button on his phone, indicating to the maid when she appeared, that she should bring more coffee.

"You look tired."

"Of course, I've been working." She looked at him. "What's your excuse?"

"Late nights. You know me, cara, after dark I prefer not to work. And early mornings, then I work."

"Well it's light and here are some ideas." She pushed the plans across the vast, polished table, accepting the coffee from the maid and taking a sip of the thick dark liquid.

He didn't pick up the papers immediately, simply took a bite out of a pastry and pushed his chair away. He walked to the French windows, opened them out and leaned against the door, inhaling the sweet warm mountain air. She had to twist in her chair to look at him. He was pleased to see she was discomfited. She glanced at the chair where he'd been sitting and pursed her lips. She wanted him back across the desk from her. He smiled to himself and didn't move.

"What have you based your ideas on?"

She twisted to face him again. "If you'd like to read through them I think they speak for themselves."

"I don't wish to. I want you to tell me."

The silk of her dress tightened across her breasts as she took a deep breath, no doubt trying to contain the anger that simmered, barely hidden, beneath the surface. "I've worked with high-profile architects based in Milan on a number of private homes a year or so ago and—"

"A year or so ago is too long. I don't want out-of-date ideas."

"The concepts are still valid, their interpretation will be up-to-the-minute. If you look at the plans…"

He took another bite of the pastry and stepped out onto the terrazza. "Later." Across the valley, with the early-morning sun barely risen from behind them, the mountains were under a shadow of blue haze. He'd forgotten how beautiful this place was. Australia, where he'd made his home, was magical and had been good to him. But for the first time he felt that tug in his gut he'd refused to acknowledge since he'd left. It was, simply, his home. He turned sharply to her.

"Come, if you really don't wish to have breakfast, then we may as well go around the castello and you can tell me your plans."

"As you wish."

WHAT SHE WISHED WAS to do her job as quickly as possible and leave. As they walked down the corridors that now buzzed with people, she mentally crunched the numbers. One month. She could do it in one month with long days and then she'd leave.

And she needed to be with him as little as possible. Whenever she was with him she struggled to retain her usual focus. She seemed to be preternaturally aware of everything about him, despite her best intentions.

Even now as he walked beside her—so casual with his tousled hair, finding its own shape after a desultory comb, hands thrust into his pockets, shirt open at the neck—she could feel his power. And in his manner too—in the way he called out greetings to people as he passed by—he had an ease she'd always envied: a wonderful, magnetic ease that drew people to him. And she was no exception. She closed her eyes briefly as he stopped outside the main reception room. She had to remember that he felt nothing for her, that all he wanted was revenge.

"Shall we start here, Isabella?"

She nodded, clutching the iPad tight to her chest. "Why not?"

He smiled—that grin again—and her stomach flipped, an instinctive reaction that she tried to counteract with the tilt of her head and clipped steps through the door that he held open.

Focus. She just had to focus.

She noted with satisfaction that Luca's staff had already cleaned the room from the previous night's gathering in honor of his grandmother. With the furniture also cleared out, only the room's bare bones remained. The battered parquet floor was in desperate need of refurbishment; the paintwork on the walls was faded and chipped and the stonework that surrounded the mullioned windows appeared dull and dingy in the morning light.

Despite her best intentions, she was distracted by Luca as he walked the length of the large room. Her gaze lingered on the muscles of his forearm as he pushed his hair back from his face and looked around appreciatively. Her eyes refused to shift from the length of his throat exposed by the upward tilt of his face as he gazed up at the vaulted ceiling.

He turned to her suddenly. "What are your plans for this room?"

She cleared her throat. "No structural change. Simply maintenance work on the floor and walls."

"And the furnishings?"

"It's a reception room. Flexible pieces that can be used for both intimate groupings and for larger functions."

"It's not a hotel I want. It's to be a family home, remember."

"The room is, as it is. If you wanted a family home perhaps you should have chosen a different property to develop."

She walked across to the windows, her footsteps ringing loudly. "We'll need some rugs—I know where to source the kind I have in mind—and paintings." She looked at the faded marks where the paintings used to hang, took a deep breath and turned to face him. "Perhaps the family portraits that have always hung there."

He snorted. "No. I'm not having your ancestors looking down on me."

"Better than your own," she snapped back.

He twisted his lips with humor. "I don't know, I think the place could do with some loosening up. An odd mix of farmers and thieves might just do the trick."

"It won't help you sell the place and that's what I thought you wanted. Anyway, I thought you said it wasn't about you; it wasn't *for* you?"

"It's not. But why would anyone want someone else's ancestors looking down on them?"

"History, continuity. They're a part of this place."

"I don't want a stuffy mausoleum."

"You won't get one. What you'd get is a beautiful room in which to receive visitors; a beautiful room to hold receptions."

"You talk of 'receiving people', 'beauty', where's the warmth?"

"If it's a 'lounge' you're after, you've hired the wrong woman."

"I've hired you. Do the job I've hired you for."

They stared at each other in a tense impasse. She shook her head, irritated, trying to pull herself back. She needed this job. She needed to communicate her vision to him. "OK. Imagine this." She closed her eyes in order to pull herself away from his presence, in order to draw on the visions that filled her heart. "You're a father, your eldest daughter is having a party."

"So? Why does she need this space?"

"No, you haven't got it yet, have you? Imagine. Twenty years time, you are a father, you're older, hopefully wiser—"

"Doubt that—"

"And your daughter enters the room. She's young and fresh, eighteen, about to leave home, about to leave you. The years of work and worry melt away when you look at her. You want, *everything* for her. You want to give her a party for everyone, to honor her, to show her how much you love her."

She inhaled sharply and looked around. "The musicians are over there and, over there," she pointed to the side, "you'll be watching her as she dances with her friends and neighbors." She looked up at the curved lines of stone that rose high above them, untouched by the morning light. "The drops of the chandeliers—crystal, I think—will bounce the light across the room, making her jewelry sparkle. And then you'll catch her eye and know that," Her voice broke and she cleared her throat, "that, everything will be all right." She stared, unseeing, across the valley, now alight with the fire of the early sun. Her eyes watered under its brilliance.

She started at his touch.

"Did that happen to you?" His voice was soft and close.

She turned to him and her breath caught in her throat. She shook her head in tight little movements. "No." She pasted a bright smile on her face. "But it should have done." She looked around. "Anyway, shall we move on?" He indicated with his arm that she should lead. She didn't catch his eye and moved swiftly out into the hall. "Let's look at the less formal rooms next. They are very old of course, but will need little change. I have swatches for fabric and upholstery." He suddenly gripped her arm, pulling her to an abrupt halt.

"Isabella, stop."

She looked away from him, trying, in vain, to halt the surge of heat that emanated from his hand, which licked across her skin, curling around and playing with her body like a lazy flame unaware of its power.

"If this is too much for you," he continued, "tell me. I can find someone else to do the job."

His kindness panicked her more than any abruptness could. Kindness would see her lose the commission. Kindness would see her sisters live without. Kindness would not ease the guilt.

"No, I'm sorry. I'm fine. Really. I was just trying to get you to see what I have in mind." She swept her hand down the silky length of her hair, a habit she reverted to whenever she felt a little lost. "I'm fine." She tried to step away but was awkwardly halted by the grip of his hand over hers.

"Are you sure?"

She nodded. "I'm sure." She had to be. "Let's move on to the other reception rooms." He sighed heavily, a look of exasperated irritation settling on his narrowed gaze and lips. She shrugged. "Unless you want to go elsewhere?"

"Si." His tone was curt as if he'd come to some kind of decision. "I want to begin on the upper floors." His gaze never left hers. "The turret room." All thoughts of his kindness fled at those words. It wasn't comfort he was trying to provide, but punishment for what had happened.

His words eradicated the lingering heat from his hand, the momentary belief at his kindness, the longing in her heart. She kept her face impassive. "Certainly."

SHE PUSHED OPEN the door to the turret room without hesitation and flicked her finger across the iPad on which she held all the information.

"A small library, I thought."

"Inspired by the bookshelves?"

"Not at all. They'll have to go."

He shook his head. "No. In my brief I clearly stated the function of this room."

"I decided a library would be most fitting."

"You decided? I told you I wanted this to be a nursery. By punching a door back through the wall—you can see where it's been filled up for some reason—it'll be close enough to the main bedroom suite. It's perfect."

"It's inconvenient."

"For whom?"

"The parents of course. They need to be there for their child."

He raised a dark eyebrow. "That's rich coming from someone whose parents—whose father in particular—did his best to keep his distance from you."

The irony of his words slammed into her gut, sending a wave of nausea sweeping through her as if she were thirteen years old once more.

"That's not true." Despite the veracity of her statement her voice sounded small.

He strode across the room. "Keep the shelves. Put the beds there," he pointed, "and a cot here. And some sort of nursery room stuff in the middle." His voice grew louder and louder and Isabella felt herself shrinking, hurting.

"I still think—"

"Well don't!"

"But I—"

"No!" This time his retort was even stronger than before. But it wasn't the words that made her stop, it was the look in his eyes. He walked toward her, circling her like an animal eyeing its prey. "Listen to me. Just listen to me, for once in your life." His eyes were fixed on hers, telling her far more than any words could. What they were talking about bore no relation to the words that were being uttered.

She swallowed the bubble of panic that rose from within and shook her head. Tentatively she reached out to him, wanting the anger to fade, wanting the aggression to dissipate. She'd spent years stepping around her father's mood swings, alert to every nuance of his personality, any sign that he would turn into the monster she hated. She knew how to calm; she knew how to evade. "I'm listening, Luca."

He stilled then and looked down at her hand, resting gently on his arm. Slowly he drew his eyes back to hers, pulled her hand from his and at that moment she was aware of the depth of his rage.

"No you're not. You never have and you never will. Not to me anyway. Your parents? Yes. It's always been about tradition, hasn't it, loyalty, doing the right thing at the right time. Well you did, and you have to live with it."

The unfairness of his accusation sparked anger. "Don't come back here and lecture me. I've lived with my actions these past seven years and will continue to do so for the rest of my life." She grabbed his arm as he turned away. "It's you, Luca, who lives your life free of the past. No pain, no fear, no vulnerabilities, how wonderful *that* must be."

He shook his head, as if in disbelief.

"Or perhaps you *are* vulnerable somewhere," Isabella continued. Luca's brow contracted fiercely and she suddenly realized how little she really knew of him. "Where, I wonder."

He swung around and slammed his hands against the wall, either side of her body. Fear gripped her. She couldn't move; she couldn't speak. But she remembered what to do: breathe. Just breathe and it would pass.

"I don't want to hear anything more about what you think. You think you know me, you think you know who I am, you think you can tell me what I should be doing, how I should behave. That is rich, cara, coming from someone as emotionally repressed as yourself."

He looked away in exasperation and she took the opportunity to slip from under his arms. Shakily she walked over to the window and opened it wide, breathing deeply of the sweet mountain air, listening to the soothing fall of the river tumbling over rocks to the valley below, just as she'd always done. Luca would never hurt her, she knew that. Only with words. He wasn't her father.

She forced herself to turn round and face him. She saw the anger had subsided, leaving confusion evident in every turn of his head, in every step he took: steps that stopped once more in front of her. She was relieved to note her panic had also subsided, giving way to the ever-present sensation of his nearness. Her breathing quickened and her gaze dropped to his lips: lips too beautiful to have uttered such harsh words.

"I'm sorry, Isabella. I'm hasty, impatient. I say things I shouldn't. But you need to know things have changed. You have to do as *I* wish now. You have no choice. That's what I'm paying you for and the sooner you realize that, the better." Confusingly he brushed away a wisp of hair that had escaped the tight French twist.

She opened her mouth but the words died on her lips as his fingers briefly caressed her neck before his hand dropped to his side. Her eyes fell to his lips once more, betraying her thoughts and feelings with each second that passed. He shook his head and moved his face closer to hers. He tilted her chin up, forcing her to look him in the eye.

"Better for whom?" Her voice was soft, shattered.

"For both of us." His voice was strong, controlled.

"You can't speak for me. You've no idea what's best for me."

It was as if she hadn't spoken, his silence asserting his disagreement. She pressed her palms against his chest, needing him to move away from her. But he didn't.

"I want a nursery here, Isabella. It's perfect for a nursery."

"No."

"Just do it."

She couldn't speak immediately in case her voice betrayed the tremor that ran throughout her body. Then she willed herself to calm. "Why is a nursery so important to you?"

His face didn't change, didn't assume an expression of victory at all. He continued to look at her as if he were trying to work her out.

"I'm going to sell this place to a family. A family would fit in well with the community and the links to Montepulciano are good. A family, Isabella. And what do families have?"

"Babies." No word emerged, just the soft plosive sound of her lips meeting twice before fading into soft sibilance.

"Babies, cots and… baby stuff. What do you think about colors?"

It felt like poison was draining through her body, turning her limbs to lead, making her heart ache and her body sick. "Colors?" She shifted, bringing one arm round her body in an awkward movement as she rubbed her opposite shoulder, shaking her head as if unable to choose from the array at her disposal. "Blue for boys and pink for girls." She repeated the clichéd pairing to buy herself time.

"Now *that* I could have gleaned from a child. *Colors*. I want you to think." His hands tightened their grip on her arms as he turned her around to face the empty room, the room that once had held so much passion, so many dreams.

A sob rose from somewhere deep inside, but she held it so tight, so hard, she had to fight for breath. She released it and inhaled deeply.

"Bright colors, I think—the primary shades of a rainbow."
He relaxed his grip on her and his hands trailed slowly down
her arms.

"Sounds more like it."

"With beautiful textures for interest. Babies love to curl
their hands around tufts of sheepskin, to push the flat of
their palms through velvet, to hold, to clench things in their
hands…"

She hadn't realized she was mimicking a baby's hand—
clenching her fist repeatedly, as if trying to grasp something
that proved elusive—until his hands curled around hers and
quieted hers, before turning her around to face him.

"You're a professional, just do it."

"You think this is easy for me? I conceived our baby in
this room. One day I left this room with my father. A few
days later I returned without my baby. You think this is
easy?"

"It was your choice." His voice was cold and distant. She
began to shake her head, to form the words of denial but the
look of cool indifference in his eyes swept her words away.
He shrugged. "It's irrelevant now." She tried once more to
speak but he held his finger to her lips. "I'm no longer
interested."

She stepped back as if struck, looking around her as if for
an answer as to how such love could have ended in such
indifference. "I have to go. I'll do as you wish but I need to go
now. I'll look at it later."

"This has priority."

"Why are you doing this, pushing me like this, Luca?"

He didn't answer immediately and part of her was glad
because instinct told her that it would be an answer she
didn't want to hear. Time had passed and he simply didn't
care for her any more.

She walked away and this time he didn't stop her. As she

pulled the door closed behind her it slipped from her grasp as the wind from the open window took it and banged it against the doorjamb. She hesitated briefly, wanting desperately to return and put things right. But she couldn't. The time had gone for that.

LUCA LISTENED to her footfall fade away. He slammed his hands against the door that still vibrated in its frame and stood absorbing the energy, using it as a counter-force to his own.

What the hell was he doing? He sank his forehead against the door in defeat. The years had fallen away and the old feelings of rejection and frustration, amplified tenfold by his body's need for her, consumed him and destroyed the tenuous peace that seven years away had brought.

She was driving him crazy.

Why? God only knew. His confusion had nothing to do with love—that had died, eaten away by the pain of her rejection.

No, he didn't know why she was driving him crazy. All he knew was that he didn't want it, he didn't need it. *Dio*! He couldn't cope with it. He needed to distance himself from her. If *she* could close down, so could he. He just had to complete his grandmother's last requests to him and Isabella to sort through her possessions, and then he'd keep away.

He pushed himself off the door and took one last look around the room where he'd thought he'd found love all those years ago. He'd been wrong. He hadn't been good enough for her then, and he wasn't now.

CHAPTER 3

"*T*ell her she's to come straight away." Luca called to his assistant as he glared at the battered tin chest that sat incongruously on his desk beside his laptop. He jumped up and walked around the desk, his eyes never leaving the chest, the contents of which were unknown.

So much for distance, Nonna wasn't even giving him that luxury.

"She says she's busy." The assistant shuffled from foot to foot in the doorway, obviously uncomfortable in his role of go-between.

Luca's eyes didn't leave the chest. "Tell her if she's not down here in two minutes I'll personally come up and bring her down, over my shoulder if I have to. Tell her—"

"Sir?"

He took a deep breath. *Control.* "No. Tell her the lawyer is insisting we follow my grandmother's last request to go through her papers together. Tell her we can't leave it any longer. Tell her…just tell her that."

Luca continued to pace behind the desk, his eyes remaining fixed on the chest that he was sure contained something sinister. Nonna was up to something. He knew it.

ISABELLA DIDN'T BOTHER KNOCKING. Just swept the door open wide as if she still owned the place. Well, she didn't.

"It's usual to knock, Isabella."

"I'd assumed, as I'd been so repeatedly summoned to you, you'd be expecting me." Her perfume hung in the air, finding a way to that part of his brain he was determined to ignore. *Dio*, give him strength. Her eyes dropped to the desk. "Nonna's tin chest."

He nodded. "My lawyer has informed me that my grandmother, in her wisdom, required us to work together on two more things: her papers and her house. I want them sorted as soon as possible. Papers today, her house tomorrow. Then we can both get on with our own work."

"Fine with me. Though I don't understand her request. She was always fastidious about paperwork. To leave these two outstanding matters…" She shrugged.

"Indeed. But there appears to be no avoiding it. I'd prefer to do it alone but apparently, Santino advises me, *that* would be dishonoring her wishes."

"Not a legal issue, surely?"

He looked up at her for the first time. "No. Not legal. Personal. I, for one, do not care to dishonor her. No matter how little I wish to carry out her request."

"Then we'd best begin."

Luca unfastened the catch, flipped open the lid and peered inside. "Looks like," he tentatively pushed his finger around its contents, "photographs. And lots of them." He sighed and only then sat down, suddenly feeling defeated.

Isabella threw him an irritated glance, leaned over and upended the chest, spilling its contents over the desk.

Photographs—all shapes and sizes, black and white, colored, some pristine and others dog-eared from much handling—smothered the papers and laptop.

He shook his head. This was going to be impossible. "I don't know why she didn't ask me to do this alone."

"Perhaps because she wasn't sure you would?"

"Of course I would. Anything legal, I'd have passed to the lawyer and, as to the personal, I'd have had it stored."

"But not looked at."

He shrugged. The personal could wait. The personal *had* to wait.

"There doesn't look to be anything official here. It's all…"

"Personal." He sighed, feeling the anger seep away leaving only resignation and emptiness. "How are we going to get through this lot, hey Isabella?"

His change in mood must have registered with her. For a brief moment he wondered how eyes of such a grey color could convey heat so effectively. But, before he came to a conclusion, the warm taupe tint in her eyes turned into the cool grey of a northern ocean with which only a fool would mess. And he was no fool.

"One at a time, I suppose," she said, her voice clipped. "And the sooner the better. I've work to do."

He took a deep breath but it didn't calm his returning irritation. The notes of her perfume seemed to meld perfectly with the scent of refreshed flowers that wafted in on the damp air through the open window.

He swept the high pile of photographs roughly across the desk: tiny black and white yellowed photographs of people and places long since forgotten mingled with color photographs of more recent decades where people stared at the camera with unfashionably straight faces and even more unfashionable clothes and haircuts.

Isabella picked up the first photograph with tentative

fingers. "I remember your grandmother showing me this one. You won the prize for the fastest sprinter in the school. She was very proud." She held it out to him, challenging him to take it, to participate.

He took it from her. "Just as well they had a prize for something like that. Now, if they'd awarded a prize for the student who made the least effort at school, there would be many more school photographs of me."

"You didn't do so badly."

"How would you know? You weren't allowed to attend the village school."

"No. But Nonna was very proud of you. She told me everything you did—good and bad."

"And I heard all about you." His eyes flicked over her, taking in the pristine hair, make-up, dress. "It used to irritate the hell out of me to hear about this virtuous girl who did everything right."

She smiled and looked down at the photo she was holding. "Not everything."

"According to Nonna you did."

"Well," she placed the photo to one side and picked up another, "even Nonna didn't know everything that went on at the castello."

The damp air suddenly felt more chill and he shivered. "What do you mean?" He swung around to face her but she didn't meet his gaze, just continued on to the next photo.

"It was lonely, that's all I mean. *I* was lonely." She picked up another photo jutting out of the pile at right angles. It was faded in the centre as if it had once been in a frame.

"Nice photo, Luca." It was a snapshot of him as a child at a village fete—laughing and engaging everyone around him in fun. "I haven't seen this one before."

"Si." He plucked it from her hand. "I remember that day. It was not long after I arrived to live here with Nonna. She had

forbidden me to go to the fete as punishment for some trans-
gression."

"And yet you went."

"Yes, I foolishly thought I'd get away with it." He dropped
the photo onto the table. "Hadn't taken into account the fact
I may get photographed."

"Was she angry?"

"Very."

"And yet the photograph has obviously been in a frame at
some point. She couldn't have been that angry."

He shrugged.

"And you always did what she said in future?"

"Rarely."

"Umm. Figures."

"What does?"

She tilted her head to one side. "Contrary. Loving someone, but unable to respect their views, their wishes."

"She understood me. She taught me right from wrong
and then let me make my own mistakes."

"And so you did."

Her implicit criticism irritated him. Always needling,
always blaming. Well, he was growing tired of it.

"Stop blaming me, Isabella."

She looked up coolly and shrugged. "I don't know what
you mean."

He leaned toward her, shifting his face into her line of
vision so that she was forced to look him in the eye. He saw
it took effort for her to return his gaze—effort and willpower
that showed in the flashes of heat that suffused her skin,
revealing the fractures in her confident exterior. "Stop
fighting me, Isabella. I'm not the enemy."

"It doesn't mean you're not dangerous," she answered
softly.

The vulnerability in her voice shot straight through him

and he reached out for her hand but stopped short. The need to break down the barrier that lay between them, to hold her so tight that she would have no choice but feel the same physical passion that simmered deep inside himself, was almost overwhelming.

Almost, but not quite. His own confusion saw to that. Because she had it wrong: it was Isabella who was dangerous. She brought all the passion, that he'd tried so desperately to lock away, to the surface. He had no idea, now, what he felt for her because that passion was overlaid and intertwined with anger at her rejection all those years ago. He had no idea what he felt and he had no wish to know.

He withdrew his hand. "Dangerous? That's ridiculous." He cleared his throat and riffled through the photos aimlessly. "I wouldn't do anything to harm you." He glanced at her. Her eyes were wide and her lips softly parted, a small frown furrowed her brow.

"Right." She raised one disbelieving eyebrow and picked up another photograph. She shifted her head slightly as if to flick away a stray strand of hair. There was none. "I'll put the photos in piles if you like. Ones for you and a few I'd like to keep if I may."

"Whatever you wish." He understood how it was going to be. Say one thing, think another. That was the way with her family.

He looked down at the photograph he was absently tapping on the table and quickly pushed it to one side. But not quickly enough. Isabella noticed and picked it up. She looked at the photo and frowned.

"I thought I'd seen most of your family photographs but I don't remember this one. It's you isn't it?"

"With that mop of hair, of course. Why do you doubt it?"

"It doesn't look like you. The expression in your eyes. You look lost and wary." She moved the photograph and her head slightly as if to gain a different perspective. "You look, actually, quite scared."

Luca flicked up his eyebrows, surprised at her perspicacity, but said nothing.

"Your father took this photograph, didn't he?"

Luca nodded.

"That's why you look so bewildered and sad."

He plucked the photo from her hand. "I was five years old when my mother died and my father re-married and decided I was surplus to requirements."

"It must have been terrible for you."

"I survived." He looked at her closely. "Curious. You're touched by the plight of a small boy who's had the only love he's known taken away from him. Yet you, yourself, willingly did the same to me."

She shook her head. "No, I didn't do that…it wasn't like that…"

"No?" He swiveled his chair jerkily from side to side, trying to contain the growing agitation as memories flooded not only his mind but also his body. He felt them viscerally. "You tell me how I should view my father cutting me adrift at the age of five years old. You tell me how I should view the woman I loved telling me to leave, not having the strength to stand up to her family for me, not loving me enough to be with me."

"I'm sorry, I—"

He held up his hand—he didn't want to hear—and jumped up and paced away, unable to contain the agitation any longer. Even with their backs to each other he sensed her confusion. A heavy silence lay between them. He took a deep breath and returned to his seat.

"But, I'm a grown man now. That boy, who believed he'd never be good enough, is long gone."

Isabella's eyes were hot upon him. He felt her gaze but

refused to meet it. He couldn't let her see his true feelings. *Dio*, he was becoming like her. Saying one thing, feeling another.

"I'm so sorry."

"Forget it. It's a long time ago."

"Your feelings have changed, then?"

"Of course. Nothing stays the same, not feelings, not people."

She fidgeted uncertainly with her fingernails. "No, of course not." She looked up at him with eyes that still asked the question.

"You want to know my feelings about being rejected by my father?"

A brief nod.

"Hurt for the boy I was, but I understand. I don't hold the pain any longer." He shifted uncomfortably in his chair, not knowing any more. This was what he'd believed. But now?

Her eyes were still fixed on him, questioning.

"You want to know my feelings about being rejected by you?"

She nodded again.

He paused, wanting to give her the answer she was seeking, but he couldn't. "I don't understand and I suppose I never will."

She looked away before he could see the full extent of her reaction. "Well, that's honest anyway."

"I've always been honest. It's you who haven't. Not with yourself."

"What do you mean?"

"You know exactly what I mean. You hide the truth, not only from others but from yourself."

"No doubt you'd prefer to believe I hide my feelings rather than admit that I have none for you." She bit her lip as if to retract the words that had tumbled defensively from her mouth.

"And no doubt it's far easier for you to carry on like this." He shrugged. "I may have changed but I haven't grown so hard, buried my feelings so deep, that I cannot feel anything."

"And that's what you believe I've done?"

"I know it, Isabella, I know it."

She stood up slowly and walked over to the window. He twisted in his chair and watched her. She couldn't bear confrontation; she couldn't bear self-examination. And he had no idea why.

She stood, silhouetted against the soft, dove-grey light, as insubstantial and ethereal as the soft gauzy damp air, and he felt an overwhelming sorrow for what might have been. He repressed it immediately—it was drowned out by what actually *had* been: his hurt, his pain. Whatever he said, the little boy who was hurting was alive and well, deep inside him.

She turned. "I have to go." Her glance shifted one way and then another. "Now. I'm sorry, Luca. I can't do this now. Another time..."

"Sure. Another time..."

Luca watched her go. Another time and they'd talk of many things; another time and they'd fill the silences with words, gestures, lies or truths; another time and he didn't know if either of them would be able to deny the powerful, primitive charge that still ran between them.

He stood up and swept the photographs back into the chest, plucking out a couple that caught his eye. He took one over to the window to see the small photograph more clearly. His finger traced the long, dark hair and smiling lips.

"Isabella, how the hell am I going to keep my hands off you?"

Suddenly he heard the sound of a casement window opening in the guest wing that projected at right angles to the main building. He saw her slender hand reach out and secure the window and then she leaned out, intent, as if searching for something, as if listening for something. What? He looked around. There was nothing, except the wind rustling in the tall trees, and the constant rush of water as it tumbled over the rocks down to the valley floor. He looked back at her again. Her eyes were closed as she pulled out the clips that fastened her hair and it tumbled down around her face, her lips falling apart as if emitting a gentle sigh. He knew then, that she'd found the sound that gave her peace. And he knew he'd been robbed of his.

He fell back against the wall, out of sight, and closed his eyes, feeling as if all the air had been punched from him. He wanted her with a physical intensity that scared him. If the past few days had proved he still hadn't forgiven her, they'd also proved his dreams of making love to Isabella weren't the product of faulty memories but were based on a powerful desire that hadn't waned with time.

And she felt the same elemental attraction too: he saw it in her eyes in her brief glances, felt it in her touch, no matter how tentative.

He walked over to the chest and was about to drop the photographs inside when he changed his mind. He opened his desk drawer and placed the photographs carefully inside, closing it slowly.

There was no future in their relationship, there was too much hurt and recrimination on both sides but, *Dio*, he was a grown man, he could find a way to endure the next few months. They'd go to Nonna's house tomorrow, as planned. But he'd keep things light, pleasant; he'd avoid the emotional. God knows he knew how to flirt, how to have fun, but for some reason Isabella stripped those abilities from him. He just had to re-find them.

CHAPTER 4

"*C*iao." Isabella waved to the mechanic as he locked her car in the garage. It wasn't due for a service until the following day but she had to get out of the castello. She couldn't spend any more time with Luca than was necessary. He unraveled her. With a bit of luck she'd be able to look over his grandmother's house before he turned up.

As she walked, she spread her fingers over the old print dress, preventing it from flipping up in the breeze. It felt like silk under her fingertips. Vintage, now, she supposed. It had been her mother's. By wearing the dress, so different to her usual clothes in its loose fit and fluid print, she was making a statement to herself, not to anyone else. Luca was wrong. He had to be wrong. She wasn't so tightly bound she couldn't feel.

She hesitated at the edge of the small sun-scorched square, fringed by towering chestnut trees whose leaves rustled and stirred in the breeze, and vainly tried to stem the wave of nostalgia that threatened to overwhelm her.

The late morning sun cast a protective light over the

valley. It was the school holidays and children played in the river by the bridge at the edge of the village; old men gathered around wooden benches outside the small bakery, drinking coffee and reminiscing, while the business of every day ebbed and flowed around them. It was still home and would always be, whether she lived there or not.

She looked up at the castello and saw the outline of a man looking down at the village from the edge of the terrazza. She walked quickly into the shadows of the shop awnings. Why had he returned? What the hell was it he wanted from her?

Revenge for the way her parents had treated him? Her father had caught them making love one night and had had a furious argument with Luca during which her father had accused Luca of being a worthless, immoral bastard, not good enough for his daughter. She remembered the look in Luca's eyes. Her father's vicious words had got to him and he'd left. And she'd let him go without a word, too scared of what her father might do. Later, after she'd discovered she was pregnant, Luca had returned but by then it had been too late.

Revenge. It must be his purpose. But he'd said not and whatever his faults, he'd always been honest.

She stopped, arrested by a sudden thought.

What if he'd returned for her? He'd not been able to keep his hands off her since he'd arrived; he'd kissed her within minutes of being with her again. And she'd responded. Like it or not, she'd responded like a woman starved of love. Which she supposed she was.

If he wanted her only for a few months, what of it? Was it so bad? They would both go their own way afterwards. She'd had years to lose the vulnerability of her youth. She was older, tougher now. The thought of submitting to those lips, those hands, his body, sent shivers of desire tracking through her body. Just a few months...

No. She continued down the street. She couldn't do it. She had to avoid him. But as she absent-mindedly greeted passers-by, the thought persisted—he must want her still. He must have come here for her. There could be no other reason he'd insisted on employing her. And, despite her best arguments to the contrary, her body stirred in response to the thought of Luca wanting her, to the thought of Luca making love to her.

ISABELLA SHIFTED her feet and gestured in myriad small ways to try to convey to the two old ladies, without being rude, that she needed to move on. But one of the women put a surprisingly steel-like grip on her arm and continued to reminisce about how charming and handsome Isabella's father had been. Isabella felt her smile stiffen on her face. Of course he had been, to most everyone else.

The old lady continued, moving both herself and her companion to tears, as she petted Isabella's arm and they moved on to their favorite subjects of death and illness in the village. Isabella wondered whether she'd ever succumb to the morose interests of the elderly. Her thoughts were interrupted by the shouts of boys and men and the laughter of women, moving like a wave toward her. It could only mean one thing.

She flicked her sunglasses down onto her nose and turned the same way the two women were now looking.

"Buongiorno signorinas! Filomena! And Luisa! Come stai?" Luca kissed both women on the cheeks and allowed them to surreptitiously feel the fine stuff of his shirt between inquisitive fingers and evaluate its cost with good humor while his eyes never left Isabella's.

"Contessa, good morning. You're early for our meeting at Nonna's house."

The old ladies clucked around him but he remained oblivious. Either that or he was very used to it.

"I thought you might like me to make a start. Save you the bother of checking through her things."

His smile was tight. "So thoughtful. However this is something she wanted us to do together. So I'll join you."

She shook her head. "No, really I—"

"Contessa," he dipped his head briefly to hers as he flashed a smile at the old ladies. "We have no choice in the matter. My grandmother requested it of us and I believe we should comply with her last wishes. Don't you think we should?" He asked the ladies who nodded in agreement, obviously rapt to witness the exchange. "You see," he linked his arm through hers as if he was afraid she'd escape, "I'm afraid you have no choice."

He pulled her away and, this time, the old ladies let them go. Isabella felt everyone's eyes upon them but Luca seemed intent only on her.

"Please don't let me keep you from your important business. I'm sure someone as wealthy as yourself can ill afford to take time from his work."

"It's nice that you concern yourself with me. But really you don't have to. Someone as wealthy as myself can afford to have people do his work for him. Most of it anyway." His grip tightened briefly on her arm and she didn't know if it was an expression of affection or control.

"How lucky for you."

"Luck, Isabella, has little to do with success."

Of course it didn't. Her need to defend herself against his charm was making her say things she didn't mean. "Look, I'm sorry. I'm sure you've worked very hard for your success. I don't mean to belittle it."

He stopped abruptly, the firm grip of his arm holding hers, pulling her to a sudden standstill. "Do you realize you've just said something pleasant to me? Progress, I think." He grinned.

She shrugged. "I guess."

"We'll be having a civilized conversation next."

"Anything's possible." She smiled back. The smile drifted away as he inclined his head close to hers. His eyes, so full of warmth and promise, drew her into their depths.

"It seems, contessa, there are rumors afoot about you and me."

Suddenly she was aware of indiscreet giggles, breaking the spell and allowing her to draw on all her willpower to pull away from his hot gaze. They started walking once more, away from the villagers and their innuendo.

"Villagers always gossip, even if there's no foundation."

"Do you believe there's no foundation? Here we are, walking arm and arm to my grandmother's house. Besides, what could be more fitting than a union between the dispossessed beautiful contessa and the wealthy prodigal son, returned?"

"You've gone your way and I've gone mine. I'll be leaving here in a few months and so will you. These people don't know the ways of the world, like we do." She withdrew her hand from his arm.

"Indeed. But, you know sometimes," he drew her hand back into his arm as they stopped outside his grandmother's house, "I wish we were innocent again."

She shivered despite the heat. "I was never innocent."

"Of course you were." He frowned. "What is it, Isabella?" His finger swept her arm and he looked hard into her eyes. "Goosebumps. Are you cold? Frightened of something?"

She shook her head and quickly withdrew her hand to

pluck the old key from her pocket. She shook her head again, more decisively this time. "I just don't want to go inside the house. It used to be such a special place for me, I can't bear to see it empty."

"Then don't. There's no hurry. It can wait until tomorrow. Do you wish to leave it?"

She bit her lip with indecision. It wasn't only that she was dreading returning to the home of her old friend. It was more than that. Nonna's house had always been her safe haven. It had been a place of comfort, where she'd been at her most relaxed. And she needed to keep up all her defenses when she was with Luca.

"I must." She lifted the key and saw that her hand was shaking. She dropped it quickly back to her side, hoping Luca hadn't seen.

"In which case, let me help." He took the key from her and fitted it into the lock, turning it until they heard the old latch retract with a solid clunk.

Suddenly she realized she couldn't do it. She placed her hand over his. "No. You're right. Let's leave it."

He grinned, locked the door once more and dropped the key into his pocket. "Good decision. The sun is high, why don't we walk away from the house, the village, the castello. Just for a while. I'd like to see if we can make it to the dizzy heights of 'civilized conversation'. What do you say?"

She shouldn't go; of course she shouldn't. But looking into his eyes she knew she had no choice. She wanted to be with him and she wanted to know why he'd returned.

THE FRESH BREEZE swept away the lingering memories as they left the last of the cottages and the castello far behind them.

"Where are we going?"

"Wherever we end up."

"But—"

"But nothing. No plans, no expectations. Let's just enjoy the sun. It's so long since I walked in the meadows round here."

Isabella blinked, trying to fight her need to know, to control. "Sure." It was only when he laughed that she realized her tight, brief reply revealed her discomfort and she pursed her lips in a vain effort to conceal her smile.

With each step away from the castello and the village, the sense of her surroundings diminished and her awareness of him grew. The uneven ground of the pasture invaded her thoughts only because he'd slipped his arm around her to prevent her stumbling. And when they arrived at the glade of tall willows whose high leaves shimmered above them in the sunlight, only some of the heat that flooded her body left, shaded from the external heat. And when she found herself at the old place beside the river she heard his sigh of satisfaction as if it were her own.

He was full of life and it was so tempting to connect to that life once more. And it seemed that he wanted to connect with her. Otherwise, why had he brought her here?

He grasped a handful of dried grass and leaned back against a tree, his fingers idly shredding the seeds of the grass and tossing them into the river, watching them as they floated away.

"Shall we stay here for a while?"

She shrugged. "Why? Do you wish to talk business? About the re-decoration and remodeling work?"

He turned to her then and his face was relaxed, his expression faintly amused, curious even. "If you wish, of course. Naturally I'll stop you once I've heard enough."

"Naturally." She sat down, tucking her legs neatly under her.

"If it's the only way I'm going to enjoy your company then I'm prepared to bend my rule of not mixing business with pleasure."

"Is it a rule you break often?"

Isabella took a deep breath of moist grassy air—tinged with the perfume of some late wild flowers—and waited for him to answer.

"No, cara, it isn't. I've never before felt the desire to put my arms around any of my business colleagues."

"And you want to now?"

"Certamente."

"Why would you want to do that?"

"Because I enjoy the feel of your bare arm under my hand. It's as simple as that."

"That sounds complicated."

"No, it's not, Isabella. You complicate things too much."

"That's because they *are* complicated." He didn't understand. And why should he?

He pushed himself off the tree and came and sat beside her. "Just for now forget about the complexity. There is just us, by the river, enjoying the peace. How much more simple could it be?"

"Perhaps for now. Perhaps for a short time I can forget." He reached out and brushed the palm of his hand lightly down her arm. "Yes, when you touch me I can forget." His fingers curled around hers until they held her in a light grip.

"Then I'd best not let you go."

She smiled and looked away. She knew the heavy burden of guilt and grief would always be there and could never be overturned. But perhaps on this glorious summer day she could have a brief respite. From his hand seemed to flow a warmth and certainty that suddenly made things very simple.

"Rest, Isabella, sit back."

She shook her head. "I'm fine." She remained with her legs tucked under her, her back straight, as she looked around. The world was peaceful under the shelter of the yellowing, sunburned leaves. Only the movement of the river stirred under the mid-day sun. "This place hasn't changed."

"No, it hasn't. But that's something a person returning should say. Not someone who has remained here."

She remained focused on the light bouncing off the water as it tumbled over moss-covered rocks. "I haven't been here for a long time."

"Nor I."

"So, Luca, tell me, why the sudden change from anger to charm? Before, you were demanding; today you are conciliatory, gentle. What exactly is it you want?" There was a long pause in which Isabella's thoughts turned full circle. He must have feelings for her; they were evident in everything he did when he was near her. Weren't they?

He laughed. "I'd forgotten how perceptive you were."

"It seems there are many things you've forgotten. Including that I know you well."

"*Knew* me well." He corrected. "Past tense; past knowledge."

"Enlighten me then."

"I always admired your directness. You want to know, you ask. Most other women would not need to know the destination before we begin. But not Isabella."

"Just call me a control freak."

"I think I have. What can I do to make you relax, to make you enjoy yourself?"

"I am enjoying myself, Luca. I'm just rusty. It's been a while…"

He reached over and picked up her hand in his. "The truth is, cara, I want to leave our past behind us. The truth is…" he hesitated, frowning before meeting her gaze, "I enjoy being with you."

It was only when she heard the words that she realized just how much she'd wanted to hear that he was here for her, because of her. He was here because he wanted to be. He didn't *need* to live here to refurbish the place. He didn't *need* to have hired her to re-design it. He was rich, powerful; his choices were vast. But he was here with her, now.

He wove his fingers between hers, slowly driving them up to their hilt before wrapping them over the back of her hand with a gentle squeeze. Then he lifted their combined fists up until they were outlined against the dappled sunlight. He released her hand, steepling his fingers between hers and she echoed the movement: touching, strong, yet separate.

"It's been too long."

"I haven't been anywhere. It's you who've been away."

His fingers claimed hers once more. "But I'm here now."

"And what is it you want now?"

Luca brought his head nearer to hers so he could breathe in her perfume and so she could feel him close. He knew she couldn't prevent the instinctive reaction she had to him. He looked down and saw her chest rise and fall more quickly and the small, delicate place on her skin, revealed by the dark upward sweep of hair, pulse rapidly. He could almost feel her opening up to him, inch by inch, like a shy bloom facing the spring after a long, hard winter.

"The same as you I think."

She tugged down her skirt over her knees with careful deliberation. "Tell me, Luca. Please."

"Ah, Isabella, if I only could." He brushed the back of

his finger down the side of her cheek and paused, waiting to see if she would speak but she sat, straight and stiff, as if unmoved by his words. "All I know is that when I touch you, I see you react and it's a mirror of my own response." He watched her body respond, more fascinated by the rise and fall of her breasts, of the bare skin of her arm, goose-bumping where his breath touched it, than trying to put into words the complexity of his feelings. He slid around so he was seated opposite to her. He could see her better now. He reached out and took her hand—so slender and refined—in his. Her only ornament was her gold Cartier watch inherited from her mother. No rings. He frowned.

"Were you never tempted to marry, Isabella? Seven years is a long time."

She looked up at him with fierce eyes. "None of your business."

She looked away again, across to the river that tumbled over the rocks in front of them. She had definitely changed. Seven years was a long time. Then, her cheeks had been softer, plumper, now they were lean and sharp. They revealed the beauty of her cheekbones. They also revealed the tension she held inside.

He loved this place but had no interest in it now; he was mesmerized by her face, watching her eyes flicker around the scene and her mouth relax under its spell. The sun caught her cheekbone, leaving the other side of her face in shadow. A beautiful face, her English coloring soft in shade and texture, dramatically counterpointed by her dark hair, again drawn back tightly from her face. Some might say a hard face. Some might, but he wouldn't, because he knew what lay beneath.

He put his hand to her chin and gently turned her to face him. "You're right of course."

What he saw stopped him in his tracks. He hadn't expected to see fear. He immediately dropped his hand.

"Cara, what are you so afraid of?"

"You, of course, Luca. *You.* What are you doing? Do you plan to seduce me, have a little fun over the next few months before you move on? Is that the idea?"

It was like a slap in the face, bringing him sharply to his senses. "I want... to be with you, without anger. I want to forget about the past. Is that too much to ask?"

She parted her lips to speak but no sound came, just a jerky intake of breath. She jumped up and walked across to the river, as if seeking reassurance in the murmur of water on rocks. "I think it might be."

He followed and took her hand. He felt the tension and some, unfathomable pain he needed to take away. "Come, Isabella. Let me hold you."

With her eyes downcast she edged her body slowly to his chest and held herself there, rigid. It was the most surprising and awkward movement he could imagine. Like a small child, unused to love, putting herself forward for comfort. He tilted her chin and kissed her gently on the lips.

"I've been wanting to do that again ever since I kissed you the day of the funeral."

Involuntarily she raised her fingers to her lips and touched them as if to reassure herself the kiss was real.

"Are you playing with me Luca? Because if you are, please don't."

He put his arms around her shoulders and pulled her to him: all needs of his own disappeared under the surprising weight of Isabella's own apparent need.

He inhaled her scent, her hair and kissed her head gently before he laid his cheek there. They stayed like that for long minutes with only the accompaniment of the birds and the river. It seemed to Luca that, rather than forgetting his past, it had crept up on him without him realizing. Visiting his old home, being with the woman he'd fallen in love with all those years ago, he'd discovered not only a woman still hurting, but also a man whose pain was undiminished.

Then she moved under his touch as if startled to find herself there and pulled away. She turned from him and wiped her arm across her eyes, again like an awkward child.

"I want to be by myself now."

He nodded. He understood because he felt the same. She remained still, so very alone, with her back to him. Then she turned to face him and he saw the utter vulnerability in her eyes.

"Tell me, Luca, just one thing before I go. You've been avoiding saying it directly. But I need to know. Why are you here? What made you return? Was it me?"

He knew what she wanted to hear. But he couldn't lie, no matter how deep her need. "I'm here because my grand-mother asked me to be here for you. She asked me to hire you for the job. She needed to know that you and your sisters would be cared for. Would be safe."

Isabella didn't understand at first. His eyes still held hers with a fierce passion, but the words told her something different.

"Oh." She stepped back. It seemed such a useless thing to say but she could think of nothing else.

"I'm sorry if that's not the answer you wanted."

She shrugged. "How would you know what I want? No, it's the truth I want and it seems you've told me that. That's all I need to know."

She began to walk away.

"Wait. Just wait a while and we'll talk."

"No." She gazed up at the leafy canopy above which

clouds gathered blocking out the sun, then back to the path that led to the castello. "It looks like rain and, besides, I've work to do. That's why you brought me here isn't it?"

"I'll see you tomorrow, then. At Nonna's."

She nodded without turning back to him. The sooner the better. She couldn't endure much more of his humiliation. One moment she thought he wanted her and the next? It was nothing but a game to him.

CHAPTER 5

*L*uca sat in the ancient wood-paneled library, shifting the pieces of paper desultorily around his desk, and wondering what the hell had happened to him in a few short days to destroy his sense of purpose. He no longer knew what he wanted; he no longer knew what he was doing. There was only one thing clear: he couldn't be with Isabella and not want her. He had to get Nonna's last request over and done with and then they could go their separate ways.

He sighed and opened the desk drawer to get the key to the house. Instead his fingers closed over the handful of photographs he'd removed from his grandmother's tin chest. He rubbed his thumbs against the edges of one, flattening the creases. It was of Isabella, at about eleven years of age, relaxed and smiling mischievously at the camera, at his grandmother. It was a smile he'd never seen, not even when he'd been her lover.

He pulled out the second photograph. She must have been a few years older—perhaps thirteen—the smile had gone and the eyes were full of distrust. What the hell had happened to wipe that beautiful smile from her face?

He frowned as he placed the photographs back in the drawer. Then he shrugged. Different photographs, different emotions, different ages. He was reading too much into it. He dropped the photographs, picked up the old key and slammed the drawer closed.

SHE WAS EARLY for her meeting with Luca at his grandmother's house.

As she waited for him in the shade of a chestnut tree, she watched him approach, phone clamped to his ear. She was about to step out from under the overhanging branches of the tree when she paused, arrested by the quiet tone of his voice. With her, he could be playful, flirtatious, angry, frustrated, but his voice always held a sense of power. But he sounded positively gentle as he farewelled his "carina" on the other end of the phone.

Then it suddenly dawned on her. Of course. Presumably he'd put his life on hold while he carried out his grandmother's wishes. So what, or who, had he left behind? Someone who inspired a gentleness that she'd never inspired, that much she knew. The thought twisted in her gut.

She stepped out into the harsh sunshine. It was none of her business. He was only here, now, with her in order to carry out his grandmother's wishes that she be provided for. No other reason.

"Isabella!" He pushed the phone hastily into his back pocket, turned the key in the lock and pushed open the heavy door.

"After you."

Isabella bit her lip and gripped her handbag more tightly, the leather straps feeling slippery in her hands.

"I could have done this alone."

"It's something we have to do together. We have no choice."

She swallowed and stepped into the stone-flagged hall-way. A wall of dry heat hit her. She tried to take a deep breath but somehow it stuck in her throat and she coughed. She stood stock still in the ancient hallway, stunned by the familiar smell of polished wood and drying herbs, of past activities that would never happen again. Over-riding the blend of fragrances was the hot, dusty smell of a closed house and a sense of grief because every-thing was the same except Nonna was no longer there. The familiar associations now pointed to a large, gaping, empty hole.

With her emotions spinning since Luca's arrival, this blast of sadness nearly undid her. She breathed deeply of the hot dry air in an effort at control and continued purposefully down to the sunny kitchen, where the old lady had spent most of her time. Luca followed close behind.

It was even hotter in there. A bead of sweat trickled down her back. She looked around, trying to ground herself in the external.

Her favorite painting—a simple, sunny still life of a vase of flowers—still hung on the chimney breast; the pendulum wall clock still ticked away the minutes and hours and the kettle still stood on the range, waiting. Her eyes fell to the wood-framed easy chair, whose homemade floral cushions were faded from the sun. It was Nonna's chair, above which now nothing moved but dust motes.

She turned to find Luca leaning against the wall looking around. As his eyes completed their search of the small room with its traditional furniture and old-fashioned kitchen fittings they rested on her and she knew his thoughts as if he'd uttered them.

"It's just a room now, isn't it?"

"Si." His footsteps rang loudly around the room that was full of things and yet felt so empty. "I came after the funeral and could still imagine she was here."

"Perhaps she was?"

"A fanciful idea for you, Isabella."

She shrugged. "It just feels so strange. The last time I was here, I was with her." She paused, remembering Luca's hastily abbreviated phone call and the anger and resentment she'd felt at his absence during the last few days of Nonna's life surged once more through her body. "Where were you then, Luca, when she needed you?"

"I was in hospital. Nonna knew about it. We said our goodbyes in Florence when she was in hospital."

She frowned. "I didn't know. She didn't say anything."

"I didn't want her to. Some things are private."

She turned away at the reminder that she now meant nothing to him.

"Of course. Are you well now?"

He smiled. "Perfectly." He paused briefly as if considering whether or not to elaborate. "I'll tell you about it some time, but not now. Not today."

"There's no need. It's your private business, as you say." She clasped the bag straps until the ridge of stitching dug into her hand, and looked around assessingly at the paint-work on the window frames, at the lime-wash on the walls, at anything impersonal that would ground her once more in the world around her.

"It's all in good order. I'm sure the real estate agent will have no problem selling it." She jumped as his hand rested on her shoulder. She hadn't known he was so close.

"Isabella, I have no intention of selling this house."

The strength drained out of her. She wanted to cry. She opened her mouth to speak but nothing emerged. She turned and tried to move away but his hand gripped her shoulder. She could have tugged away. She could have slapped away his hand. But her feet seemed bolted to the floor. All she could do was shake her head.

"Then what the hell is this all about?" She drew in a shuddering breath.

"You know what it's about. Nonna wanted it. She didn't know I wasn't going to sell. She wanted us here, together." He shook his head. "There's no understanding her. There never was."

"So, what are you going to do with it. Are you going to redevelop?" She turned to him then, back on familiar ground. "Do you want ideas?"

There was a long pause during which the rush of energy ebbed away under the onslaught of a gaze that revealed nothing of his thoughts. He shrugged carelessly. "Why not." He walked over to the kitchen and leaned back against the cupboards, they pressed inwards with his weight. There was something so relaxed about his stance that she had no doubt it was something he'd done thousands of times over the years, perhaps while he talked to his grandmother while she cooked. "OK. Tell me what you think about the kitchen."

She forced herself to concentrate. Her eyes glossed over the wood-fired oven, the source of so many loaves of crusty bread, so many dinners. "Depends. For anyone who'd want a real kitchen, yes, of course, it's satisfactory."

"Satisfactory." The soft tone of the repeated word struck a loud note inside her. What was he doing?

"You know it is. It's perfectly fine. It can cater for a small family or large gatherings."

"Or, rather, Nonna could."

She looked down to avoid his gaze. "Yes. Nonna could."

He sighed heavily. "She told me you were a frequent visitor here after I left home for university."

"I must have been about thirteen when I first came." She swept a finger across the top of the stove and rubbed the dust between her fingers. She continued to focus on her fingers even though the fine grey dust was no longer there. "My father didn't like me coming to the village. But I used to sneak away to see Nonna." She glanced up at Luca warily.

"Of course. She was a loving woman. When I came to her as a boy I was doing what you're doing now—going through the motions, day by day."

"You're mistaken. That's not what I'm doing."

He shrugged. "I was. I was just waiting and hoping I would come out the other side."

"And you did survive. Because of your grandmother."

"Only because of her: her belief in me, her love for me. Tell me, Isabella, who do you have?"

Startled, she walked to the centre of the room and straightened the bowl at the centre of the well-worn oak table that contained the miscellaneous pieces—paper-clips, coins, curled-up stamps and a beautiful glass button—that all kitchens seem to collect.

"I don't need anyone. If I did, then of course I have my sisters."

"Your sisters, for whom you care so much. I hope they're grateful for your sacrifice. What are they doing at the moment?"

"Portia's at University and Karina is in her last year at college. I employ their old nanny to keep an eye on them. They're probably old enough to care for themselves, but I worry about them."

"Of course you do. You always have. But, you know, I bet they're having fun, going out, flirting, being young. While you waste your life away worrying about them, doing everything for them."

"It's not like that. They're my responsibility."

"It seems everything is your responsibility. And, you know? It's not, Isabella. It's not."

"Luca." Her voice was quiet and restrained and polite. "I think perhaps we've fulfilled Nonna's wish now, don't you?"

He looked away as if defeated. When he raised his gaze to hers once more he appeared weary and withdrawn. "Just tell me if there's anything you want here. A keepsake maybe?"

Her eyes shot straight to the painting. His gaze followed hers. "The painting? It's worthless. A local artist I think."

She walked over to it. Her fingers rose to touch but stopped, half way.

"I've always loved it."

"You want it?"

"I'd like it very much."

Her interest seemed to have stirred his own and he looked up at her with a piercing gaze.

"It's yours. But what do you see in it?"

She opened her mouth to speak but no words emerged. Instead her eyes searched the familiar shapes and shades of the painting. Every brushstroke, every highlight had been ingrained on her since she—a child in a woman's body—had started seeking out the comfort of her old nurse. And she wanted to release herself to the balm of that comfort now. It wasn't just a colorful painting of a vase of flowers, it was a device that took away her pain.

"I see forgetfulness."

"Forgetfulness? Is that the way to move forward? To forget the past? You need to move on, Isabella and I don't think forgetting is going to help you."

Anger sparked inside her. "What right have you, Luca? What right have you to try to bring up the past?"

"The right of an old friend."

Tears of rage sprung to her eyes at the epithet that was a pale shadow of what she felt for him. Even now.

"That's it. I'm off." She picked up her bag and took one step, but he was beside her in an instant, his hand firm on her arm. She looked down at it, feeling the anger, the impatience, the passion mounting with each passing second. "Take you hand away." Her voice was trembling.

"No."

"Why?'

"Because you keep running away. This will be the third time you've run from me, from your past. And how's that working for you, hey Isabella? Is that making life easier for you. Don't you think it's about time you faced up to things?"

She flung his hand away and turned on him furiously, her whole body shaking with rage and something more.

"You want me to open up to *you*, hey? How dare you Luca? How dare you come back here after all these years and make these demands of me? You use Nonna's wishes as an excuse to try to break me down—"

He threw his hands in the air. "Hey, I'm not trying to—"

"Don't deny it. You think it all so simple. You think you know me; you think you have an idea of what is going on inside me and you have none. *None!*"

"It doesn't take a genius to see you won't face things, to see you keep running from your past, keep reinforcing those barriers."

"You say *I* have barriers. What about yours? At least I know mine exist. You're not even aware of why you're doing this." She hesitated briefly at the sudden look of bewilderment on his face. "I do. What you want is to play with me." She was so close, his breath was hot upon her face. A muscle in his jaw flickered with tension, his lips were suddenly next to hers. Energy sparked through every vein in her body, through every nerve cell and across her hot skin.

Before she even knew what she was doing she'd plunged her fingers roughly into his hair and around the back of his head until she held him in a firm grip. She pulled his mouth to hers, pressing her lips against his with all the passion that ferocious longing—and just as ferocious denial—could bring. She captured his mouth with one swift flick of her tongue against his lips.

It was as if she'd lit the touch paper to an explosion. His lust ignited—as strong and primitive as her own—and he took control, demanded it. His tongue slid against hers, pushing into her mouth and pushing away all thought; his fingers dug into the sweat-slicked small of her back; her hands pulled him hard against her.

Their mouths moved against each other's in a kiss that held no tenderness, only a savage desperation. His pressure against her body was too much and she stumbled back against the kitchen table, a chair falling over with a clatter.

She briefly felt the ridge of the table hard against her bottom before his hands slipped between her and the table, creating a buffer against which he leaned as she lay back flat on the table, pulling him down on top of her.

The bowl, and all its contents, went flying. It smashed on the floor, but they were both too far beyond reach to respond. There was only each other, held against each other. And, still there was too much separation.

He ground his body against hers and she lifted her hips to his. Her hands pushed up under his shirt, seeking a connection with the taut muscles that shifted under her touch as his body sought satisfaction. His hands slid down the sides of her tight-fitting dress and up her bare legs until the tight dress prevented any further progress.

He grunted with frustration as her hands pushed under

the belt of his jeans, pulling him tighter to her as the soles of her feet rubbed against his legs.

But her dress was too tight; there was no room to move.

Frustrated and breathless they broke their kiss. Slowly reality inserted itself between them, and the sound of the prolonged spinning of a coin seemed preternaturally loud before it settled with a clatter. They both looked across at the pieces that lay scattered over the floor, including the beautiful glass button that lay shattered on the hard tiles.

Their faces and bodies were so close and yet the distance had never felt greater. She closed her eyes against the destruction and shook her head. "No." Her voice was almost too soft to be heard, too soft to be a word. He tried to collect her in his arms again but she wriggled from under his embrace. "No." Stronger, this time. She needed that distance; she couldn't have it any other way. She'd do anything to protect herself. Even lie. "Is this what you wanted? Is this what you really wanted? A quick fuck on the kitchen table?"

He winced at her uncharacteristic choice of words and didn't move for several long moments as his eyes searched her face—what for, she didn't know. Whatever it was, he obviously didn't find it and he shook his head. "No." His voice was as soft as her words had been hard.

"No. Well I can't do more than that." She shook her head, suddenly defeated, picked up her bag that had fallen to the floor and looked helplessly around at the mess. She shook her head as she tried to smooth back the hair that had tumbled from its clips under his fevered embrace. She couldn't stay to pick up the pieces. She just couldn't. She turned and walked toward the door.

"Don't go, Isabella." There was no pleading tone in his voice but equally no command. She stopped but didn't turn to face him.

"I have to."

"Look, ask me again, if I want you here and now. My 'no' was probably hasty, more than probably, inaccurate."

She heard the shift in tone, the underlying humor as he tried to break the tension between them. She turned to him and shook her head.

"Stupid question for a man, I guess."

"Stay."

"I have to go. Don't you understand?"

"I understand more than you know."

"Then let me be." He didn't reply and she didn't face him. "Please."

"Of course." Too quickly stated, too curtly uttered. Another pause. "Although, it was *you* who made the first move. Perhaps I should be asking you to let *me* be."

"Perhaps you should." She shook her head in confusion. "Look, a few months and then I'll be gone. It's not long. We can do this."

She took one last look around the room and opened the door.

"Where are you going?"

"Away from you."

"It's not over. You know that."

She stopped and turned round slowly feeling the truth and yet the falsehood of his words at the same time. It wasn't over but it *had* to be over, for both their sakes. "Yes, Luca, it is. It was over long ago, when my father sent you away." Her heart broke a little. "When I let you go."

"You didn't know what you were doing. You wanted me…" All humor had vanished now as his voice trailed away into the labyrinth of his own deep-seated insecurity.

Her heart seemed to stop then and she realized, as if from a distance, that she couldn't afford to feel any more. Ice spread slowly, cauterizing the ache.

She shook her head. "I wanted you to go then, just as I want you to go now. Unfortunately you are my boss and I need the money. So, if you can find a way to make these few months as painless as possible for the two of us, that would be appreciated."

He swept his hands wide in disbelief. "How can you stand there and speak so coldly after what just happened?"

"That was our bodies talking. That was sex. That's nothing to do with true feelings. Don't get the two things confused."

"Cara, I don't. I'd be crazy to feel anything for someone as cold as you. And I'm not crazy. You're right. There's no future for us."

"And no present either."

She didn't look back as she strode down the hot, dark passage, just heard the scrape of the chair as he picked it up off the floor.

ISABELLA RETURNED IMMEDIATELY to the road, back to the path that led to the castello. She walked without stopping, without noticing the people smile and call out greetings, oblivious to the heat of the sun that scarcely registered above the inferno that raged within.

Why the hell didn't Luca just leave things alone? There was no way anything would change now. Too much had happened. Only a heavy lust existed where once love had been. It was all too complicated to resurrect.

She focused on placing one elegantly shod foot in front of the other on the uneven cobbled path to the castello. She knew, by experience, where to place her feet. She knew the uneven places, the broken places and she knew to avoid them. So when her ankle twisted on one of the ancient stones, split where a cart had shed its load decades before, she could have cried with frustration. She knew, and yet she'd fallen.

She gripped the stone wall for support as she rotated her ankle—dimly grateful it wasn't painful—and looked out across the valley. She couldn't see the river from here, hidden as it was by rocky outcrops and the village but she knew it was there. She could hear its roar as it passed out of the valley, through a narrow gully and plunged hundreds of meters into the valley below. She'd lived with the sound as a background witness to her life for years. But now she drew her hands to her ears, unable to stand it and walked away.

Once inside the guest suite, she pulled the door shut behind her and closed her eyes. It was quiet here. Thank heaven. This part of the castello was scheduled for redecoration later. Even so, she didn't feel quiet. There was enough noise going on in her head, in her heart, to deafen the sharpest of hearing.

Wearily she sat down at her desk. Her hand reached for the electronic pen and computer pad and the screen flicked into life before her.

This was real: the regular lines on the grid, the flashing cursor awaiting her command. This was her reality, the future she could control. She opened the design of the room she was currently working on and picked up the pen. She hesitated only for a moment, before the pen descended driven by something other than feeling and she exhaled her frustration.

The pen became an extension of her hand and she was soon engrossed in the intricacies of making something beautiful. Difficult minutes flowed into absorbed hours as she forced herself to focus, to retreat once more from the world of feeling into the world of form.

CHAPTER 6

The castello was silent except for Luca's impatient footsteps, pacing back and forth on the terrazza. Fireworks burst into the night sky marking the beginning of the Ferragosto celebrations. Whoops and shrieks of laughter drifted up to him from the village where everyone gathered: everyone except for him and Isabella. For what did they have to celebrate?

He turned and paced again.

Dio! What had he done?

One minute she was hot against his mouth and he'd felt, for a split second, not that time had rolled back, but that he'd pushed forward beyond the barriers into the world that had haunted his dreams for so long. The next? The past had replayed and he was back where he started.

Except for the longing for her deep in his body. Except for the frustration and anger that ground into the pit of his gut.

She'd retreated once more.

He was angry with himself for allowing his need for her to surface. God knows why he did it. Pure impulse, he supposed. The reason he did everything. He'd always been ruled by impulse, acted on instinct. It had served him well in business. And had failed him abysmally in his private life.

The massive hall clock struck eleven, the sound echoing through the empty rooms, emphasizing the days that had elapsed since he'd last seen her. She'd somehow managed to avoid him and he'd not sought her out.

He pushed his hands through his hair. Why should he let her affect him? He was here for one reason only. To follow his grandmother's wishes to make sure Isabella was cared for. She'd do the work, he'd sell the castello. They'd both achieve what they'd come here to do. And then they'd go their own separate ways again.

A burst of fireworks—brilliant golds, reds and greens—filled the night sky and the smell of sulphur drifted across to him.

He couldn't begin to be the boy he'd once been. That person was long gone. The hope and trust and love that had filled that young boy's heart had disintegrated into nothing, just like the fireworks. The time for love was past.

He needed to move on. Energy jolted through his veins. He hadn't settled since they'd last seen each other. He needed to do something. Progress was moving well on all areas of the house, except one: the conversion of the turret room into a nursery. Nothing had been done there yet.

He turned suddenly to the guest wing where a single light indicated Isabella's presence. It was next door to the turret room.

He needed to move on and he knew where to start.

~

CONCENTRATING on the technical drawings was difficult enough for Isabella, without the rhythmic thud that had just begun somewhere close by. She frowned, her hand clutching, too tightly, the pen above the design pad. Whatever the source of the noise it was nothing to do with her.

She focused once more on the free-hand strokes but her concentration broke when an almighty thump vibrated through the solid walls.

What the hell was going on?

She glanced at her watch. It was nearly midnight. Everyone was down in the village celebrating Ferragosto. No-one should be working.

She walked down the deserted corridor following the noise until she reached the turret room. She opened the door and saw Luca, in jeans and a tight t-shirt, dismantling the bookshelves.

It took a minute to find her voice. With the noise he was making, he was unaware of her and she couldn't take shift her gaze from the muscles that bunched in his arm. Her eyes traveled up and around the broad shoulders, following the line of his muscles as they tightened across his back as he inserted the crow bar against the wall and prized the end of the bookshelf away from the wall. With one almighty splitting sound the side of the bookshelf flew out. He dropped the crow bar, picked up a sledgehammer, and turned. She noticed he didn't look surprised to see her.

"Interesting way to refurbish. Destroy first."

"Just carrying out orders, contessa. Get rid of the graffiti. The carving was too deep to plane back so I was going to replace it but the top's split."

"Get rid of it then."

He let the sledgehammer fall to the floor with a thud and leaned against the wall, his arms crossed.

"You've no feeling for any of this, have you?"

"They're bookshelves. And mine no longer. There's no

room for sentiment in business. There's nothing personal about this."

He pushed himself away and walked up to her. She stood motionless. Isabella watched, fascinated as a muscle in Luca's jaw moved, just as his eyes narrowed.

"Is that so?" He brought his head close to her, his eyes never straying from her own. His eyes were filled with anger and frustration. Their honey brown was darkened as if the sugar had been burned off leaving a gray charcoal gloss. "What makes it personal, cara, is how you react to me. The chemistry between us is what makes this personal."

"Chemistry! Chemistry isn't of any use to me. I don't *want* chemistry." She raised her face to his in defiance, her nose almost touching his cheek. "I don't *need* chemistry." The tension in his body released in a shudder of warm breath upon her face.

"You may not want it but it's there. Deny it all you like, but it's there all right."

"And what the hell good would it do, if I did open up old wounds, to examine them, to expose them, only to find—"

"What, cara. Only to find what?"

"Nothing. Only to find, nothing."

She moved away and smoothed her hair that was tied tightly on top of her head in a sleek ponytail.

"And what if you do see something there?"

"There is nothing to see, Luca." She ostentatiously flicked a look at her wrist watch. "It's late and I'd appreciate it if you left this until tomorrow. I've work to do and you're disturbing me."

"I think I need to remind you of something, contessa." Again he drew near but this time his face had softened, his lips quirked in amusement.

"And what is it that you find so amusing?"

"You. You're my employee. You work for me. You do as I say, not the other way round."

"And that's exactly what I'm trying to do. Work." She pushed her hand against his chest in an effort to move him out of her way. But he was immovable. "Now if you'll excuse me, I have work to do, money to earn."

"Sure." He stepped aside. "How long can you keep up this cold façade?"

She turned at the door. "Indefinitely. It's who I am. I'm here for business only. I don't care about anything else. No sentiment." She pointed to the bookcases. "Those? They hold no affection for me. No memories I wish to recall. Get rid of them if you can't fix them properly."

As the door closed behind her there was an almighty crash as the sledgehammer hit the wood, followed by loud swearing. She winced. He'd taken her at her word. She rubbed her chest with the heel of her hand. She hadn't meant it. Hadn't meant any of it. And it tore her up that he'd believe her to be so unfeeling as to want to destroy something that had given her such comfort of the years. Just prosaic items, but the shelves brought back the memories of times spent together. Intimate times. Times she was desperate to forget but couldn't. She wanted to go inside and tell him. She leaned her forehead shakily against the door.

Suddenly the door opened and Isabella fell against him, her hands slapping against his tightly muscled, shirtless body. She jumped back.

"I was just about to come in. I heard what you did."

"What I did was nearly cut my finger off. You make me hasty, Isabella."

She looked down and saw that his t-shirt was tightly wrapped around his hand. Despite that, blood had soaked through it and was dripping down onto the floor.

"*Dio!* Show me."

"No. It needs stitches. I know that much."

"Hospital. I'll get someone to drive you there."

"*You* can drive me there."

"No. It's the hospital. I can't. I'll have someone drive you."

"There is no-one, Isabella. They're all in the village."

"OK." She gulped down the rising panic. "Where are the keys?"

She had to keep a clear head. She had to get help. Even if it meant going to the one place she still had nightmares about.

"In my pocket."

She stared him in the eye while she plunged her hand in his jeans' pocket and felt for the keys. The pockets were deep and Isabella closed her eyes, knowing that a blush swept her face. "You're not losing that much blood then."

"It would take a lot for me not to react to such a touch, Isabella." She hooked the ring through her finger and dragged the key ring out. "I could have used my left hand you know."

"Then why didn't you?" she snapped.

"Seemed like too good an opportunity." He smiled. "For both of us."

"Watch it, Luca, otherwise you'll be bleeding to death here. And let me tell you blood is impossible to get out of unstained wood."

"Ever the designer."

He put his arm lightly around her and pulled her to him briefly in a hug designed to reassure. And it did. She shook the car keys in her hands. "Let's go."

Isabella looked up from the gear stick she was studying and glanced across to Luca's hand.

"Wrap it up more tightly, the blood's coming through."

He grunted as he tied another swathe of cloth tightly around it. "Don't worry about me, just drive." He tied the knot with his teeth and left hand and frowned. "First gear is here." Isabella stuck her foot on the clutch and he moved it into gear for her.

"Thank you."

"Do you know the way?"

"Believe me, I know where the hospital is."

They lurched around the driveway and sped suddenly down the steep drive.

"Perhaps I should have asked if you know how to drive."

Isabella glared at him. "Of course I do. But in my Fiat. Not this *thing*. If the Fiat weren't in the village garage now, I'd be driving it."

Isabella slammed her foot on the clutch as she approached a tight bend, bashing the gear stick with the heel of her fist, trying to find the higher gear.

"This *thing* is a Lamborghini."

"Whatever it is, it's stupid." She bashed again, the car made a graunching sound.

He placed his hand over hers and maneuvered the stick into position. "Now release the clutch before we take out the wall of that house."

She did and the car bounced over the edge of the pavement.

"Stop. I'll get someone in the village to drive me."

Isabella kept on driving.

"I said 'stop.'"

"No. We can't afford the time. You're beginning to look pale."

Silence fell between them as Isabella sped down the mountain pass and joined the main road into Montepulciano.

As they entered the outskirts of the town the tension

increased in line with the traffic. Buildings grew taller, hemming them in, higher on either side of the narrow streets as the traffic speed slowed. The traffic slowed further and stopped.

A clammy chill swept her body. She looked into the rear-view mirror and saw nothing out of place except a light sheen on her pale face. It should have reassured her. If she could keep the panic in then all would be well.

"I can't think why you always need to drive, when you drive so badly."

His very calmness infuriated her further. "I don't drive badly." She checked her rear view mirror again for reassurance.

"Of course not. Checking your make-up is exactly what rear-view mirrors are for."

She gripped the wheel. "I know that. And I *am* a good driver. Just not today. Not with you." She muttered under her breath.

He turned to her, not looking in the least perturbed by the fact the engine was straining now in the lower gear. Isabella didn't want to risk changing gears again.

"Of course, it's my fault. Like so many things."

"Well if you'd have kept your eyes on what you were doing, we'd never have to be speeding to casualty."

"And that, cara, is your fault. It's proving impossible to concentrate when I'm near you."

Her heart thudded and a fire swept through her body that added to her tension. "You should have employed someone to do it."

"Some things are personal. You know that."

She shook her head. "Stop it Luca, this is too difficult." The tears were pricking now and her eyes were beginning to mist.

"What is it?" He hooked a tendril of hair behind her ear.

They were coming closer now.

"Nothing." She swallowed the lump in her throat, trying to control her mounting hysteria.

She wouldn't think about it. She wouldn't look at the only new black wrought iron posts that marked the place of her accident. She'd just drive past swiftly—even if it was in third gear—and not look at the place where her dreams had died.

"Hey, what's this? It's a Ferragosto procession. Slow down, Isabella."

Isabella had no choice. They drove up the main street, the shops and cafes teeming with people. The old railings that separated the street from the footpath were ornately designed, except for one stretch that they were slowly approaching. Then they stopped, people milling all around them.

"It doesn't look as though we'll be going far for a while, there's people stretching up the road. At least my hand's stopped bleeding." He turned to her then. "Isabella, my God, what ever is the matter?"

They'd stopped directly beside the place where her father had crashed the car seven years earlier. Her eyes were fixed on the railings that didn't fit in with the old ones.

Isabella felt the tears threaten inside her and then freeze. She stared at the railings but didn't see them. She saw only memories: vivid and bloody. Her father's head, the steering wheel pressed into it; the blood flowing from it and the seat belt that she'd worn, wrenching into her belly, blood flowing from between her legs.

"Christ! Get out of the car! Blood or no blood, I'll take over."

He jumped out of the car and she absently followed his movement until her gaze rested on the blood that smeared the handle from his cut. He came round and opened her door and grabbed hold of her hand. "Isabella, get out of the car."

She looked up at him and shook her head but did as he said and stepped out and walked round to the other side in a daze.

With him in the driver's seat, they sat for a few moments until the crowds cleared. "Are you going to tell me what that was all about?"

She opened her mouth to speak but no sound emerged. Her mind was filled with the horror of that day, seven years before, when she'd lost her child in an accident that had also killed her father. The two were inextricably linked in her mind. A part of herself had died that day.

She shook her head, leaned back and closed her eyes.

Eventually the car moved slowly off and within five minutes they were at the hospital. She opened her eyes and turned to Luca.

"I'm sorry. I…"

He brought his good hand to her cheek. "I'm not leaving you until you tell me what that was all about." Then he got out, walked around to her side and opened the door for her.

If it hadn't been for his good hand curled around her waist, she wouldn't have made it through the hospital doors that she still remembered. That day, seven years ago, when her world had collapsed, her shocked senses had noted the pale green doors and the smooth plaster of the walls, had studied the ornate ceilings of the private hospital as she'd lain back and allowed the doctors to do what they needed to do. While she did what she needed to do and studied the form of everything around her, her eyes and mind gliding along the patterns, colors and textures of the ceiling rose inset with functional, institutional lights. She'd thought at the time she'd have done them differently. Just before she lost consciousness.

Now she was dimly aware of Luca insisting that she sit

with him and of a nurse seating her in a corner of the examination room and pressing a hot drink into her hand.

She watched as Luca's hand was cleaned, stitched and freshly bandaged. What she didn't watch was Luca's face because she knew he hadn't taken his eyes off her.

As soon as the nurse left, Luca came and sat beside her. She looked down at his bandaged hand. "She did a neat job with the stitches."

"I'm not interested in my hand."

"You should be."

"Damn it, Isabella. I want to know what happened out there today. You didn't look as if you'd seen a ghost, but as if he'd coming running at you with a knife."

She blanched at the accuracy of his words. "I suppose I did." She took a sip of her drink. "I guess you weren't aware of where the accident took place."

"Your father's accident? No."

"It was there, where the new railings are."

"*Dio*! I'm sorry, I didn't know. All I knew was what your mother told me. That you were returning from the hospital —from the abortion clinic of the hospital."

Isabella closed her eyes tight against the pain of her mother's betrayal. "She told you that?"

"She took great pleasure in telling me that."

Isabella nodded and took another sip. She opened her mouth to speak but her throat felt parched despite the liquid. "I'm sorry, I didn't know she'd told you that. That would have been my mother trying to hurt *me*, by hurting *you*."

"What?" His brow contracted in confusion.

She shrugged. "We weren't close. There were," she searched around the room vainly for words that could possibly convey the complex relationship she'd had with her mother, but finding none she closed her eyes. It seemed easier to talk that way. "There were other things that happened that drove us apart. And I'm sorry. I—"

"Too late to be sorry, Isabella. It's done. You did what your parents wanted and had the abortion."

His words drove down deep like a barbed dagger, destroying all that lay in its path, taking with it all hope of retrieval. How could you forgive someone who'd lied—even a lie of omission—all these years?

The silence had driven him to his feet. She watched as he paced like a caged animal, stopping at the windows, below which the Ferragosto festivities continued. His shoulders were tense. She realized then that the dagger had cauterized in some way, killed the rot.

She rose and came behind him. He took her hand and placed it over his heart without looking at her. The lights of the town were reflected in his dark eyes, which looked so far away. "I missed that child, Isabella. I missed her. I wanted her." He paused and she swore that neither breathed. "But *you* didn't." His last words came out in a rush of exhaled breath as if he didn't want them inside him. Didn't want to face the thought that she'd aborted their child.

"It wasn't like that." She swallowed back the tears. She had to force herself to tell him, to face the pain for his sake, to give him some peace.

He pulled her to him. "Whatever your reasoning, it's done. It's over. I blamed you at first—was angry—but I shouldn't have. Everyone has their reasons for their actions and I should have respected yours." He lifted her face to his. "I would have told you that if you'd let me see you. Tell me, why wouldn't you let me see you?"

He frowned as he brushed away her tears.

"We were on our way there," the words tumbled out in a rush and she gasped to get her breath, "to the abortion clinic."

"Yes, your mother took great delight in telling me you'd had an abortion."

"But I didn't, Luca, I didn't." Her words were like a soft moan of regret. "Don't you hear what I'm saying? We were on our *way* there, not returning."

He grabbed both her arms. "Tell me."

"My father discovered you'd returned and told me we were going to Montepulciano to see you. Turned out he was lying. When he told me where we were really going, I went crazy. Screamed, shook him. In the end he simply said that he would rather see me dead than see me with you. I watched as he swerved into the fence."

"You were on your way there?"

"Yes."

"Then, the baby?"

"Died from my injuries."

She literally saw the shock slam into him: his body jolted, his mouth opened as if to speak but no words came, his eyes widened and then closed as he brought her hands to his closed eyes and held them there for a long moment.

"I'm sorry. I'm so sorry." Then he let her hands fall.

This was it. This was the moment when he'd walk away. She'd let Luca believe a lie: Luca, a man to whom honesty was everything.

But instead he pulled her to him and held her in his arms. He stroked her hair down its length—again and again—but she couldn't relax, just held herself stiffly waiting for the rejection. Instead he pressed a kiss to her forehead before he pulled away but she held her eyes fast shut. He cupped her cheeks with both hands and kissed her eyelids. Only then did she open her eyes to look at him. Was the impossible happening?

"I'm so sorry. But, cara, why didn't you tell me something like that? Why didn't Nonna tell me?"

She lowered her head. "She didn't know. No-one knew."

He shook his head in disbelief. "Why? Why did you want me to believe that you'd aborted our child?"

She shrugged. "I was numb. I couldn't think straight."

"But then later. You could have told me at any time."

She pressed her lips together as if to stop any words, and shook her head, feeling helpless to reply. How could she tell him what she'd been through in one sentence? She sucked in a breath. She needed to say something. She owed him. "I'm sorry, Luca. I just couldn't have. I can't explain." She looked into his eyes that revealed both sorrow and hurt. "My child was dead."

"*Our* child, Isabella, *our* child."

"Please, Luca, you must understand."

He shook his head and she felt the tension in the slight movement that contained a world of meaning. "I don't understand."

Panic rose inside her. "You must. What difference would it have made if I'd told you?"

"All the difference in the world."

There was a knock at the door and a nurse entered.

Luca picked up the car keys. "We must go."

CHAPTER 7

*T*he lights flickered as he drove fast along the motorway toward the castello like so many years passing him by, fleeting, insubstantial. Except the difference was that the years had left their mark.

His belief that Isabella had aborted their child had led to a series of events and consequences: some of which he couldn't regret, some of which would be even harder to tell her about now.

He glanced at her but saw only her profile that looked eerily colorless in the regular flashes from the street lights.

And that she hadn't trusted him with the truth? He gripped the steering wheel tightly with his bandaged hand and winced. What could that mean, but that she had been rejecting him, wanting him to believe the worst of her, pushing him away. Again.

He flexed his cut hand in the bandage and rested it once more on the steering wheel. At least his fingers were agile enough to maneuver the gearstick. He couldn't have taken another ride like the first and it gave him something he could concentrate on. He pressed his foot hard against the accelerator, needing the speed of the car to drown out the confusion that raged inside and that he was helpless to express.

He turned off the motorway and began the long climb up the winding roads with its hairpin bends that would take them up to the small village and the Castello Romitorio: Romitorio or retreat. And so it had been for the monks who'd originally lived there, followed by miscreant royals wishing to be close to the city but far enough away to retreat to a defensible home. No wonder Isabella had found it safer to stay there over the years.

He looked over at her and felt instant guilt. He'd been roaring around the bends with his usual abandon, forgetting Isabella's fear of being driven. She was using her legs to wedge her in securely. One hand clung to the door handle and the other one clasped the edge of her seat.

He was scaring the hell out of her. He slowed down, taking the bends more carefully and sensed her relax a little. But only a little. He knew she would never recover from the car crash. But he also knew he wouldn't now, either.

He might not be left with vivid memories or physical scars, but Isabella—the one person he'd believed in and loved without question—had lied to him and rejected him, as surely as his parents had.

He slowed the car as he went through the now deserted village and then up the narrow drive to the castello where he swung the car into the driveway with a last-minute show of power and pulled on the brake hard.

"Luca…"

He didn't answer, just turned to her. What he saw in her face shocked him. He'd not seen behind the mask, and the poignant mix of grief and confusion hit him in the gut. He turned away, unable to face her and she opened the door, obviously believing that he wouldn't or couldn't speak with her. She was right. He couldn't. Not yet. Because he didn't know how to tell her what he needed to tell her.

He followed her into the castello. The lights were on. The staff had returned. Everything was normal. Everything was different.

"Luca, please, talk to me. Tell me what you're thinking, tell me what you're feeling."

He turned to face her. He felt as if he were looking at her down the wrong end of a telescope, she seemed so distant. He reached out and traced the line of her face, lingering on her jaw. "Not now, Isabella." He brought her to him and held her briefly, trying to tell her by his embrace what he couldn't tell her in words. He closed his eyes against the barrage of emotion that assailed him.

He now knew what she'd gone through—the full extent of her pain—and he hadn't been there when she needed him. But he also felt her lie, her lack of faith in him, like a wash of suffocating oil lying on the surface of his feelings, stifling them, depriving them of life. "I can't. Not now."

He watched her walk, head held high, her back stiff and straight. He rubbed his temple with the heel of his hand, wanting the pounding to stop. But it didn't. Seven years of believing a falsehood. So much had happened because of that lie, so much which had led him to where he now stood, unable to run after her and hold her and make everything all right. He shook his head, turned and walked away.

~

HE WOULD SEE HER. He *would* listen to her.

Isabella had kept the truth close to her for years. No-one knew. Her mother had guessed, Nonna may have suspected, but no-one else knew for certain. But now she had to tell Luca.

If he was disgusted, if he walked away and she never saw him again, then so be it. He could think what he liked of her, but he *would* hear her out. He *would* listen to her. She couldn't continue the lies her father had begun so many years before.

THE CASTELLO WAS alive with people. Masons repairing stonework that she'd had no money to fix. Carpenters, electricians, builders, hammering, sanding, chipping away at the years of neglect, bringing the castello back to life again. Just like her, Isabella thought ruefully. She'd changed more in the last few weeks than in the previous seven years. And it was down to Luca. She owed him the truth. And she owed it to herself too.

She greeted the assistant who had a desk in the small room beside the library. To her surprise he immediately jumped up and stood before the door.

"Apologies contessa. Signore has left specific instructions that no-one, on any account, is to disturb him today."

She smiled tightly, controlling her hurt. He didn't want to see her.

"Of course. Thank you."

She turned away but instead of returning to the main castello she went toward the rear where the servants' quarters were.

He was making it difficult for her. That was fine. But he would see her. The willpower that she depended on formed a solid knot in her stomach. *She could do this.*

She stepped outside onto the terrazza. It was deserted but a quick glance half way along the wall showed her what she'd anticipated. The library doors were flung open to let in the soft mountain breeze. She walked quietly up to the door and was about to knock when she stopped, her hand arrested at the sight of him. His fingers were spiked through his hair and he had his head gripped in his hands, his eyes closed tight. It wasn't the relaxed look of a tired man, it was a man in the depths of despair.

She knocked at the window. "Luca?"

He didn't even bother to move his hands, simply tilted his head up to hers, a weary smile rested on his lips. "Isabella." He didn't seem surprised to see her.

"I'd like a few minutes of your time."

He stood up but didn't move to her. "Please, come in, take a seat. I was going to see you," he looked down at the large tidy pile of papers, obviously untouched since his assistant had deposited them there, "after I'd finished this lot."

Their eyes locked. It was an excuse and they both knew it.

She smiled tentatively and stepped into the room, now so different to when it had been hers. Gone were the old ornaments, antiquities, paintings, books. In their place were sundry photos of people and families she didn't know, a few gadgets and little else.

He waved his hand for her to sit. She sat forward on the leather chair and met his gaze full on.

She tried to utter the words she'd rehearsed. Alone, with only her thoughts and memories, the idea of revealing to Luca the feelings she kept buried had seemed possible. But here, under the ambiguity of his complex gaze, her convictions slipped away.

"You had something you wanted to say to me?" His tone was gentle, encouraging.

"Yes, I…"

An understanding smile quirked the corners of his mouth. "It's difficult, no?"

She nodded.

"I don't want to make it any more difficult than it is. What can I do to help?"

"You can listen."

He sat back in his chair, his head resting on its back as if he hadn't slept for a week. "I'm listening."

"Thank you." She lowered her gaze to his lips on which a slight smile rested. She didn't need to see his eyes to know what he was thinking—his mouth was just as expressive. It was now resigned but receptive. The thought encouraged her. "It wasn't easy for me, Luca." His lips parted as if to speak but no words were uttered immediately. She swallowed.

"Go on."

"When you entered my life I thought 'this is it'. I thought 'this is my opportunity to break free.'"

His lips hardened then as if dealt a blow. "That was all I was for you? An opportunity to get away from your family?"

She shook her head. "No, of course not. I," she hesitated as she groped for the right word, "I felt so much for you—I'd never had a proper boyfriend. You were so gentle, so loving, so different..." Isabella hadn't known that someone could frown with their lips. She drew in a deep breath. "So different. You showed me what was possible between a man and a woman."

"I should have been more responsible and looked after you better. You should never have fallen pregnant."

"You did look after me, after that first time. But that was all it took. And I had no regrets."

"You didn't?"

"No, how could you think it? I'd always wanted children. Always. I love my sisters and care for them now as my mother would have done if she were still alive. And I would have cared for our own, Luca—with or without you—if the baby had lived."

He jumped up, paced away from her before stopping abruptly and turning to face her. "You see, Isabella. *This* is what you should have told me. Seven years ago. Why didn't you?"

She sucked in a long, deep breath. "They couldn't get me out of the car immediately because of the way the door had buckled and I was trapped. But they saw my father was more seriously injured than me and they tried to get him out while I watched. They didn't know he'd died and I couldn't tell them because I couldn't speak. So I watched as they tried to raise his head from the steering wheel. But the wheel was too deeply embedded. I..."

She broke off and his arm was around her shoulders. "Don't go into details."

"No, I must. I want you to know how I felt when I watched all this. I knew that my child had died because it came away from me while I was trapped in the car. And I knew my father had died. Only I was alive. And only I was responsible."

"You weren't responsible."

"Oh, but I was." She looked calmly at him. "You see my father was jealous of you. If he couldn't have me then no-one else could. And I was too ashamed to tell you."

The hand on her shoulder froze. "What did he do to you?" His words too, sounded frozen solid, as if they emerged in perfect chunks, devoid of emotion, each one separated from the other.

"The details are unimportant and not so salacious as to attract tabloid attention. But there was enough touching, enough innuendoes, enough inappropriate behavior to make a very young girl know, right from before she should have known about such things, that her father thought of her in a different way." She cleared her throat. "Whether it was the whisky to blame, or... I don't know... But I'd smell the alcohol fumes and know that..."

She pressed her lips together in a grimace of pain, trying

to suppress the feelings that threatened to bubble forth. The pain felt unending and bottomless and she feared that if she ever gave way to it she wouldn't be able to stop. She turned away from him then and pressed her fingers between her eyes, rubbing them as if to expunge the pain. She gulped a shallow breath of air and slowly let her hand drop. Then she turned, reassured that her features were schooled into an impassive mask once more.

"*Dio!*" His hand dragged away from her just as she'd feared it might. But she couldn't stop it. She'd feared he might feel repugnance toward her and she understood. After all that was exactly how she felt.

"I felt guilt, Luca, not just because I felt responsible for the death of my father. I felt guilt because I was glad he was dead."

He pulled her to him. She batted away his hand but he held her close. She hit him again. "Did you hear what I said? I was *glad*. It meant I wouldn't have to live with it any longer. Glad." She sobbed and squeezed her eyes shut. She was scared that once she started to cry she'd never stop. She pushed him away again and this time he left her. The strength she needed returned as he moved away.

She opened her eyes and was relieved to find them dry. "Of course my mother hated me for the attention my father gave me."

"She knew? The bitch knew about this?" She'd never seen Luca this angry before and she flinched under the attack, even though it wasn't directed at her.

She shook her head. "No. I don't know. She must have known something but we were a family who kept things quiet, who made sure they appeared to be doing the right thing."

"When all along your father was—" Luca turned and

thumped the wall with his fist. "Bastard. I should have killed him when I had the chance."

"There was no need, Luca. I killed him. I knew he was on a knife's edge and I goaded him about you. For the first time I'd defeated him. I had the power and I used it. You can't believe the number of times I'd wished him dead."

He came and knelt before her, taking her hands in his own. "I think I can." His voice was gentle.

"Don't you see? I killed him. I knew he couldn't bear it and I went on and on at him until he saw the railings and swerved into them. I lived. But I also died."

He looked up at her suddenly, his eyes so close to hers, they seemed to look directly into her soul.

"You wanted me to hate you. You wanted me to reject you. You wanted to be punished."

She nodded jerkily. "I suppose so. Something like that. Some kind of bargain with God. A penance: if I leave Luca then I'll pay for my sins. Whatever, I certainly didn't feel I deserved to live. I'd killed a man. If he hadn't been a good father to me, he'd been a good father to my sisters and husband to my mother. I'd deprived them of their life, of their security."

"Your father was in debt. To my father. You know that now. Your family's lifestyle was on borrowed time. It always had to end."

"I know. And I'm grateful for what you've done. Buying the castello when I had to put it up for sale."

"My grandmother."

"Ah..."

"It's all over now. You've a chance for a new life."

"It'll never be over, Luca. Don't you understand? Some things are permanent."

She saw he was puzzled, his brows drawn close. He shook

his head once, mutely asking her to explain but she couldn't. Not yet.

"The penance is paid. You no longer have to avoid me." He strode across to her. "Don't you understand, Isabella?" He held her shoulders too tightly. "It's over. I'm here now. Look at me. Really look. There is nothing to be gained by avoiding me any longer."

She felt ancient—as if she were a generation older than him—looking at him from the perspective of pain and experience. She had to push him away. He would have no future with her. She had nothing to give him.

"You seem to be working on the assumption that I'm avoiding you to hurt myself. You're wrong." He felt the depth of cold and hurt in her eyes. "I'm avoiding you because I don't wish to be with you."

He pushed her away, stepping back as if struck.

"Then what the hell was this all about? Why tell me?" He came close and she saw the sharp taste of hurt in his mouth, the way his lip curled, the way his eyes flamed in defense.

"You deserved an explanation. That's all."

She stood up but his hands stopped her from walking away.

"That's not all. Not by a long way. You're still holding back on me. I will get through to you Isabella. If it's the last thing I do."

"It was the last thing my father did."

She walked quickly out the door, much to the surprise of the clerk, before Luca could see her tears.

Isabella was reluctant to leave the quiet of her room where she'd spent the rest of the day. Here she could hide from the world, hide from Luca. She'd spoken the truth. She didn't wish to be with him. He embodied everything that she'd once wanted and everything that she now knew was out of her reach. She would never be that happily married woman with a large family. It would never happen and she owed Luca enough to not hold out any empty promises to him.

It seemed Luca had anticipated her reluctance and he'd sent a maid to her with an invitation.

"Signore Vittori would like you to join him on the terrazza for a drink."

Isabella glanced at her watch. Early for a drink but she had to face him some time.

When Isabella saw him she stepped back instinctively. He had his back to her and had just emerged from the swimming pool. Water ran down his tanned back, slickly outlining the muscles, taut from recent use. His legs were long and lean and his shorts clung to his bottom. He turned suddenly as if somehow aware of her, although she hadn't made a sound.

Their eyes met and he smiled. Isabella had to use all her powers to keep her gaze on his face and not lower.

"Swim first? Or drink?"

"I rarely swim."

"A drink then." He turned to pour her a glass of champagne.

"Juice please."

He continued to pour the wine.

"Shame you don't swim. It's a good pool now I've had it refitted. You should try it some time."

Isabella shrugged. "I don't have time. I'm always too busy for such things."

"So what do you do for pleasure?"

"Luca, remember yesterday? What bit of 'I don't want to be with you' don't you understand?"

He grinned. "All of it. Now answer my question. What do you do for pleasure?"

She shook her head in defeat, charmed despite her best intentions. "My work is my pleasure."

"And that, cara, is why I wanted to see you."

He handed her a glass of champagne.

"I also rarely drink alcohol."

"So many things you don't do. Perhaps now is the time to try a few things?"

She looked down at the effervescent liquid and realized that the residual flutter of fear she'd always felt at the sight and smell of alcohol—the trigger for her father's unwanted attentions—was there no longer. She accepted the glass.

"After you have drunk this glass of champagne I want you to return to your room and pack a bag. We have some traveling to do."

"You may. But I have work to do. And, in case you haven't noticed, that work is here."

He touched her under the chin and smiled. "Cara, I don't wish to pull rank but I am the one paying your wages."

She took a sip of champagne to hide her confusion and coughed a little as the bubbles caught in her throat. "At the moment you don't look much like a boss."

"Is that right? And why is that?" What was it about his smile, the way it seemed to work from her insides out, teasing and melting?

"You're hardly dressed."

"I'm glad that you are not accustomed to bosses in a state of undress. I find that very reassuring."

He snaked an arm around her and drew her closer to him. She shivered under his wet embrace.

"And for another, you are very wet."

The lowering sun skimmed over his bronzed skin. She

closed her eyes at the smell of him and breathed deeply. Then she got a grip on herself and pulled away.

"And now you are wet too, I think."

She narrowed her eyes at his innuendo and she took another sip. The champagne seemed to slip down easier now. She couldn't remember the last time she'd drunk any. She sat down facing the setting sun and watched as he roughly dried himself and beckoned for the maid to bring some food.

He passed her a piece of crostini. Her mouth watered. She took it and ate it, washing it down with another sip of champagne. She sighed and sat back, letting her sunglasses slip down onto her nose. "So, are you going to tell me where we're going?"

His shadow fell on her as he sat opposite. "Now where would the fun be in that?"

She sighed and opened her eyes. "You and your fun. I thought you said this was business."

"So it is. But we both need to get away from here for a bit. Away from the memories."

"There's no point in running. They're part of both of us. We can't run from them."

"Then you should address them."

"That will do nothing. We just need to carry on."

"And tomorrow we will carry on elsewhere. I want to show you a very different kind of house. I think you'll appreciate its beauty, its modernity. Are you ready to go?"

She looked down at herself, frowning. "I'm not prepared. I had not anticipated—"

"'Prepared', 'anticipated', come Isabella when was the last time you did something spontaneous?"

"I need to plan to do something spontaneous."

"I rest my case. Call it a business trip to provide inspiration."

"I don't need inspiration. You don't think I'm up to the job?"

He laughed. "I love it when you're angry. Your face is flushed and your eyes are darkened. Just like—"

"I can leave now if you like. Leave the castello, leave the job." She stood up. "You've done what your grandmother asked of you. No doubt there are plenty of other people with the required inspiration."

"Sit down. Finish your drink and stop acting like a child."

She opened her mouth to speak but he'd robbed her not only of words, but of any coherent thought whatsoever. She'd always been the responsible adult: the one who gave structure to her family's life. She wasn't used to being talked down to but, as she replayed her words in her head, she couldn't help but see his point. She sat down.

"We both need to move out from the shadows of the castello." He looked up at its façade. "It's a beautiful building and will be a beautiful home. But we need a perspective that can only be gained from a distance."

"Perspective." She mused, setting down her champagne flute. She didn't usually muse, but the champagne seemed to be taking effect. "Perspective isn't something I've been able to achieve in a while."

"You've been too involved, unable to look at things clearly. Will you come?"

He leaned forward and picked up both her hands in his, studying them rather than her, his thumbs rubbing her fists as if deep in thought. Then he pulled them to his lips and kissed them gently, raising his eyes to hers as he did so.

The words she was going to say literally melted away under the touch of his lips. Her heart pounded and sensations skittered chaotically through her body. Although he dropped her hands from his lips, he continued to hold them within his own, his fingers massaging the tendons with a firmness and repetition that betrayed his doubts. Instead of the planned remonstrations she heard herself say "OK."

The stroking of her hand stopped and it was his turn to look disconcerted. "OK? Isabella. You've just agreed with me!"

She grinned. "Yes. Now all you have to do is tell me where we're going."

CHAPTER 8

*O*f course he didn't tell her.

But, with the distant brilliance of the white-topped waves that spiked the electric blue of the Atlantic Ocean spread out far below her, she had a good idea. She sat back in her seat to face Luca who immediately leaned forward, his eyes searching hers with a smile that made the missing years between them melt away.

Since she'd told him about her father she'd felt much closer to him. She hadn't imagined that. She'd assumed she was only telling him the truth because she owed him. Because she regretted the pain she'd caused him. She'd not imagined for one moment that it would make her feel any different. But holding a secret—a humiliating secret—close to you for so many years, letting it eat into your soul, was as corrosive as rust on steel. It devoured you from the inside. And yet, now, it was as if the rust had fallen away, leaving something fresh, new and tender: something alive that she hadn't even known to still exist.

"Worked it out yet?" His voice was low and teasing.

She raised an eyebrow. "Maybe."

But she couldn't contain the grin that slowly spread across her face in response to his challenge. And she couldn't prevent the shift in awareness created by his move toward her. His knees were close to hers; his hands, that were clasped lightly together, were a whisper away from her own.

She saw the same awareness in his eyes that narrowed on hers. Without moving his hands he extended his finger and stroked hers. Such a light touch, barely any effort on his part, but its effect on her was anything but light.

"So tell me where you think we're going."

She swallowed hard in a vain effort to control the sensations that sang through her body, finding their home deep inside her. "I think I've just stopped thinking."

"Interesting." He moved his hand a little so his finger could explore the inside of her wrist. While the touch was gentle, barely there, it felt as intimate as if he'd kissed her. Her gaze instantly dropped to his lips, which curled into a knowing smile.

"Why interesting?"

"Because I usually like a woman to think. But somehow, watching you 'not think', watching your reaction as I touch you so lightly, makes me want to touch you more." His finger moved firmly up the centre of her arm until it nudged under the tight edge of the sleeve of her top where she clamped it with her hand and took a deep breath.

"The States?"

The curl to his lips straightened out into a wide grin as he sat back, taking away his touch, depriving her of its heat.

"Correct. I want to show you some of the houses I've worked on. One in particular. Have you meet some people too."

"Who?"

He turned away abruptly, but not before she caught a glimpse of the smile in his eyes suddenly change, lose its flirtatious humor and shift into something deeper and warmer. "You'll find out soon enough."

"So many secrets, Luca."

He looked at her again, the smile now replaced by a frown.

"Just unknowns, Isabella. Something unknown can only be called a 'secret' if the other person cares. If not, then it's simply something not known. Which would it be to you?"

She shrugged, trying to convey an indifference she didn't feel out of habit. But she was anything but indifferent as the impact of his words destroyed the mood, like an unseen object dropping onto the surface of calm water: radiating out waves of alarm across its surface and triggering something much deeper below the surface.

He sighed, rose and left the cabin.

She turned back to the window and gazed across the intense blue to the distant dark-edged land feeling numb once more.

He had secrets.

She'd revealed her worst secret to him. She'd laid herself bare to him. But she knew little of what he'd been doing since he'd left Italy. He'd become extremely wealthy, married and divorced, that much she knew. But, despite his wealth and charisma, he'd somehow managed to avoid the gossip columns and she knew little else. And there was a look in his eyes just then: a flood of warmth that alerted her to something that he held close, that he held dear. Something she knew nothing about.

It was a "secret" all right and yes, she did care.

THE HELICOPTER CIRCLED around the top of the building, revealing giddying glimpses of the giant grey slick of the

Hudson, the buildings, staggered in size and unreal, like some giant 3-D model, all interspersed, far below, with criss-cross streets, swarming with cars and people.

Once they landed, the door was swept open and Isabella was assailed by noise: from the rushing of the helicopter blades, to the roar of the traffic far below and the sirens whose wails seemed to fill the skies. Luca jumped out first, took her hand and she hesitated to jump down into this world that she could hardly believe was real. But before she knew it he'd taken her by the waist and swung her out of the helicopter and into his arms.

For one giddying moment Isabella felt the wind whip around her and the world tipped and spun and she staggered. But she was quickly grounded as he pulled her to him in a quick hug and brought his lips to her ear.

"You're safe. I have you."

She leaned into his body and knew he was right, whatever secrets he might hold.

It was only an hour's drive out of New York but it had shed some of the hustle. But not all. Sleek cars cruised the highway and behind high walls she glimpsed grand houses that opened directly onto the beach.

The Hamptons. She'd heard about it—a playground for the rich and famous—and now here she was. She glanced at Luca.

"A jet pilot, a helicopter pilot, why not a chauffeur?"

He glanced at her in mock seriousness. "I've had one recent bad experience of being driven around. It reminded me why I always drive myself. I don't intend to make the same error again."

"I only crunched the gears a little."

"A lot. And whether the engine will ever recover from your reluctance to move out of third gear, is anyone's guess."

"Hey, I'm sorry. I had other things on my mind. I'll pay for the damage."

"I am teasing, *mia tresuro*."

"Well don't," she pouted as she swiped his arm with the back of her hand. But her playful gesture turned into something else when he caught it with his free hand, his eyes never leaving the road and brought her hand to his lips and kissed it.

"But I like to tease you." He brought her closed hand and rubbed it against his faintly stubbly chin, the roughness resonating through her body.

"Why?"

He turned off the highway toward the beach and stopped briefly to allow some gates to slide back before pulling up before a huge glass building, that seemed to hover over sand dunes. Only then did he look at her.

"I tease you because I love to see you as you are now. Your face flushed, your mouth slightly open and your eyes wide as if waiting in delicious anticipation."

He pulled on the handbrake and then leaned over and brought her face to his. "Isabella, *mia cara*." His words felt like a caress against her skin. "We've arrived."

It was only when his face, still close to hers, broke out in a wide smile that she realized his words weren't some kind of recognition that their relationship had shifted to another level but were simply a straightforward matter of fact.

She looked up at the wall of windows and blinked. "Where exactly?"

"My home."

He jumped out of the car and opened the door for her. The morning sun lit the whole house, reflecting its brilliance so that it shone like a multi-faceted gemstone.

"This is yours?"

He unlocked the front door and indicated she should enter.

"I bought it some time ago to help a friend out. I'll sell it back to him when he's ready. But I use it from time to time. Come on I want to show you around; I want to show you a home that has no history."

"I can't imagine such a thing."

"And that is why, *cara*, I've brought you here."

"To turn my back on my history? That's impossible."

"The fact is it's been a hell of a few weeks and I think we could both do with a break. Let's pretend, just for today, that we're old friends with no history. A clean slate; a new beginning."

"I'll try." She looked around the cool white interior that reflected only light, no shadows, no places for memories of any kind to hide. "A place where darkness doesn't linger. Interesting."

"Nowhere to hide. I thought you might like it." He placed a hand on the small of her back. "Shall we?"

The interior was sleek and minimal with all the focus on the modernist lines of the rooms and the views across the slim patch of grass-covered dunes down to the ocean that roared at their feet. It gave the impression the house was a boat on the ocean. She walked over to the window.

"That view is the decor in this house."

He walked up behind her. "It was. But you're here now. I thought this house would suit you and it does."

She turned to him. "You think the castello doesn't suit me?"

"I think it's a burden."

"It was my home."

"It was an albatross around your neck."

She smiled. "Such a strange expression."

"After years of living in Australia, I have many stranger ones at my disposal. Would you like to hear them?"

She laughed and raised her hand. "No, really. I can imagine."

"That's better. You've been too tightly coiled. Come, I've arranged lunch on the deck."

There were no staff around but people had obviously arrived, set out a feast of local delicacies and left again. She sat down and accepted the glass of champagne. It felt like years since she'd been entertained like this.

"To you, Isabella," he held up the glass in a toast. "Thank you for being with my grandmother, thank you for loving her and caring for her."

His words slipped into her unawares and stirred her sadness with the soft touch of tenderness. With deliberate movements she sipped the champagne, focusing on the dry, effervescent liquid as it lay on her tongue, before slipping down her throat; focusing on the physical in an attempt to stave off the tears that sprang in response to his words.

"No need for thanks. I owed everything to her. She was the only person who ever showed me love."

"The only one?"

She hid her confusion by taking another sip before answering. "You know what I mean."

He sat down opposite her and leaned forward as if observing her. "I'm beginning to think I hardly know you at all."

"We were together for such a brief time."

He didn't reply but looked away as if her words had touched him. But how could they? It had been Luca who'd left her. If he'd really loved her like he'd said, he'd have waited for her to recover from the accident.

When he turned to her again she saw the warmth in his

eyes. "I'm sorry, Isabella. Sorry for not waiting and not understanding. I was too young, too hot-headed."

She opened her mouth to speak but he held up a finger to her lips. "And I'm sorry for bringing our past up. Today isn't about past. It's about now."

SHE CLOSED her eyes against the mid afternoon sun and allowed herself to succumb to the deep relaxation that came from good food, good wine and seductive company. Not only seductive but magical. Because somehow, in the course of lunch, Luca had managed to make her forget her past and grief. All there was, was him and now.

"Luca, you're a bad influence. I should be working."

"You should be doing whatever I ask you to do."

She opened her eyes to meet his and suddenly realized she'd drunk more champagne than she'd intended. Either that or something had shifted subtly in their relationship. Before her was a man who promised everything in his eyes.

"You wish."

He sat back, his eyes hooded, his lips, that curled into the suggestion of a kiss, looked indecently sexual. "Yes, I do."

She narrowed her eyes in confusion. "Luca, this," she waved her hand around the intimate setting, "all of this, flirtation with me. What's it all about? Our relationship ended a long time ago. You bought the castello from me. And now you want me is that it? Just admit what it is you want."

"What I've always wanted. You."

She swallowed nervously, afraid to probe further to find out if it was a brief affair he was after, or something more. Because if it was something more he wanted, she had nothing to give him. She sucked in a long breath of salty air and exhaled slowly.

"Yes, right. That must be why you got married." She wished she hadn't said the words as she watched the brightness in his eyes fade. "Your grandmother told me."

"What else did she tell you?"

"Nothing. What else was there to tell?"

"Not now. Come, I'll show you round the rest of the house." Secrets again. But they could wait. She owed him that.

They walked slowly through the huge house, one room melting into another. It seemed to go on forever, but it was the outside that drew Isabella. She lingered on one of the decks while Luca took a phone call. The sea crashed—white and sparkling, onto the sandy shore, dragging the tiny grains into itself, pounding them until they grew smaller still—mesmerizing her.

"Cara," Luca smiled as he watched her. "I have some phone calls to make. I'll leave you to it. Look around, relax and experience what it feels like to live somewhere like this. I want to give you some inspiration."

Leaning back against the railings, his curling hair blowing in the soft breeze, he looked impossibly young, handsome and carefree.

"You have." But probably not how he thought.

He stepped in front of her, tilted her chin and kissed her gently on the lips. "We'll meet up later. I have some things I need to attend to."

"Sure." She watched him walk away before she returned to the main living area. She pulled her camera out of her bag and began doing as he'd suggested, wandering from room to room, awed despite herself.

It was palatial: rooms that appeared to have no ending melted into an infinity pool that stretched, seemingly to the shore, a brighter blue than the cerulean blue of the ocean. Isabella pushed open the doors and stood, transfixed, fascinated by the shimmering light coming from the sea and ruffled pool, and by the palest straw of the grasses that grew in the dunes. It was all so light and easy and fresh.

She kicked off her shoes, sat on the edge of the pool and dangled her legs in the cool water. She didn't know how long she sat there but eventually she rose, lifted her camera to her eye, scanned around and began taking photos. She clicked her camera every time she moved her head and the light on objects altered: bleached wood carved by the sea one way, palest underside of a blade of grass captured by the breeze another. She stepped down onto the boardwalk, taking photos, close ups of the grasses, sand and the sparkle of the waves as they crashed onto the beach.

Then she turned to where the study wing jutted out onto the deck and she saw Luca standing there, watching her. She shivered suddenly, aware of every centimeter of her skin, of how her hair had teased out of its knot and of the sand that stuck to her wet legs, shoes long since abandoned. How long had he been watching her? Instinctively, almost as a sense of protection, Isabella drew her camera to her face and focused on his face and clicked the shutter.

It took a few seconds and by the time she'd let the camera fall, Luca had returned to his desk and his laptop, apparently absorbed. Suddenly Isabella felt drained and tired. Jet lag, she told herself. Nothing to do with the fact that she reacted like a puppet in his hands. One look from him set her body and mind in turmoil.

She returned to the informal sitting room and sat down on one of the cream, suede couches that dominated the space and began flicking through the photos. She'd captured something in them—a sense of peace—that had escaped her for a very long time. Then she moved on to the photos of Luca, commanding within the white frame of the open window. The sun shone on him directly, casting no shadow. The breeze had swept his hair back from his face. She clicked on the zoom, bringing his face into closer focus. And again. And again. What she hadn't seen, until now, was the expression in his eyes.

LUCA LOST TRACK OF TIME. The longer evenings meant that the sun was only now dipping below the horizon, casting a golden glow over Isabella. He sat and watched her. Asleep her face was soft and sweet: the Isabella he remembered. Her lips were fuller and it was all he could do not to go over to her and press his own to hers. As it was, the sight of her dress —soft and feminine for once—resting high up on her thighs, had forced him to resort to placing a light cover over her—to keep her warm and to give him some element of peace.

He thought of what she'd done—or not done—all evening. And with each passing minute had realized that all this sensitive woman had done was to retreat from the world that had proved too difficult for her. And his impatience with her, his lack of understanding as to the depth of her grief had led to their separation. She'd spent the last seven years punishing herself for her father's and child's deaths as she conscientiously looked after her sisters, giving them the life that she would never now have.

His grandmother had been wickedly perceptive.

Isabella moved in her sleep, taking a deep breath as she arched her neck, twisting her head sensuously into the cushions, as if enjoying the sensations of the silky material against her face and head. She licked her lips and, although her eyes were still closed, he knew she was awake.

"You know, Luca. I can sense you there, even though you make no sound. Even though I can't see you."

Her voice was husky and low, hardly heard but felt deeply in his body, stirring him, drawing him to her.

"And how is that, Isabella? Perhaps you're a witch?"

She smiled and opened her eyes.

"Maybe. It would explain a lot."

"Yes, it would."

He could still see the soft haze of her dreams in her eyes. They mesmerized him. Right at that moment he truly believed her to be a witch. It was all he could do not to go to her. He wove his fingers together tightly and twisted the heels of his palms against each other. He would control himself. There was too much to be said, too much between them, to simply jump on her like an over-sexed youth. He stood up, frozen for one moment and then walked away, aware that her smile had faded.

He noticed his hand shook slightly as he poured two glasses of wine. What was it about Isabella that cut through the years of success and made him feel like a boy again? *Stupido.* By the time he'd returned she'd swung her legs around and sat with her legs crossed defensively. He couldn't blame her. He handed her a glass.

"Salute!"

"Salute!"

A rectangle of light shifted down like a chequerboard across the white walls, catching Isabella in its lower right third.

He sat down opposite. "You're framed. Like a picture."

"Is that how you see me? As some kind of dead image, devoid of life?"

He paused, considering her answer. "That's how you've been for the past seven years. A static memory, an image that would come upon me when I least expected it."

She raised her eyebrows in query.

"At night usually." He took a hasty sip of his wine and jumped up again as if he'd been stung. And he had in a way, he thought, as he paced away through the open windows and out onto the deck scanning the horizon restlessly—stung by the bitter-sweet nature of his memories.

"Hope they weren't unpleasant dreams."

He looked down briefly, gripping the rail of the deck, before turning to her as she walked up and leaned against the open door.

"I haven't stopped thinking about you for years. I don't mean to. I don't want to. Whenever you enter my thoughts during the day I can block them. But at night?"

He lowered his head while still retaining a firm grip on the railing. He gripped it like a lifeline that would keep him from slipping into the abyss to which she always called him, where he could lose himself forever. He turned around to find her standing close beside him.

"But at night," Isabella continued where Luca had left off. "At night, you have no chance. At night the body is taken over, your mind can do nothing but watch and regret."

His hands were hurting, white against the rail. "But we're here, together, now."

She looked down and gently curled her fingers around his. "Just for a few months and then you'll be gone again."

He shrugged. "No-one knows what the future holds. You can't control it. Why don't you stop trying and trust your instincts for once."

Her hand trembled over his and he slipped his hands over hers so she couldn't let go.

"You were always so much better at that than me."

"What are your instincts telling you now?"

She didn't speak immediately and he knew he was going to receive a half-truth.

"They're telling me many things. But I'm only prepared to listen to some of them."

He heaved a ragged sigh as he felt the silk of her hair brush against his cheek.

"*Dio*! I hope they're the same instincts that are calling to me at this moment." He slipped his arm around her and drew her to him until the fresh citrusy smell of her hair and the faint remnants of her perfume filled his lungs. His heart thudded in his chest, wanting her so much, but not wanting to take what didn't belong to him. Despite what he wanted, her needs were paramount. It had to come from her. "Are they?"

CHAPTER 9

*I*sabella moved her lips, trying to form the words that were proving elusive. God, her brain was proving elusive, so close to Luca. Instead, she stepped away. He frowned briefly until she smiled, a smile she hoped would convey what her instincts were telling her. She continued to walk and pull him behind her, down the steps that led to the beach. He followed her, their pace increasing until he stopped and touched her hair.

"Your hair, it's falling out of its knot."

She didn't bother to touch it. Simply held his gaze and shook her head, allowing the remainder of the hair to escape. "I don't think I'm going to win this one."

He stepped down onto the sand ahead of her, his body a dark silhouette against the remaining light. She was aware of a restrained sense of power: in his stance and in his hand as he took hold of hers. He knew what he wanted and knew he was going to get it. He pulled her down off the boardwalk and onto the sand.

"My shoes…"

"Take them off."

A thrill at his short command shot through her body and she slipped out of them. She wriggled her feet in the soft abrasive sand, relishing its chill against her soft skin.

The breeze was warm but strong and, as they walked along, she couldn't take her eyes off Luca's body: his white shirt glowed in the dusk, clinging to his muscles, flat against his chest and shoulders and billowing out behind.

She slipped an arm around his waist, her fingers searching beneath the loose shirt for his warm skin. He reacted immediately. She felt the intensity of his eyes upon her as if they were a bright light exposing her. She couldn't meet his gaze and looked out to the sea—dark except for the wind-whipped surface—and imagined what he was seeing.

"You know, Luca, I never understood what you saw in me."

He stopped in his tracks, his grip on her hand complete. "Stop, Isabella, look at me." He pushed his fingers into her hair, loosening it further from its bindings and held her head firmly. "I see now what I saw. A girl who is sharp and clever, a girl who is sensitive and loving, a girl for whom my body yearns. But I see something else now which pains me."

"What is that?"

"A girl who's hurt. It destroys me to not be able to take away that hurt."

A dry, empty sob rent through her body, cracking and dissolving all remaining doubt and she turned to him, not able to sustain the emotional distance between them any longer. His lips met hers with a fierce heat that drove everything from her mind, everything but the need to feel more. All the frustrations, hurt and anger were powered into the intensity of their mouths moving, one upon another, almost devouring in their urgency to find each other and to taste each other.

Luca was the first to pull away, his hands moving from

her shoulder blades down into the small of her back and lower. His hands dipped down to the back of her thighs where he scooped up the diaphanous dress and shifted his hands up under it, heating the bare skin of her legs before settling around her bottom where he pulled her to him.

"Cara, I want you." His words were spoken against her skin; his hot breath sent shivers running down the length of her body, corresponding to the wet heat within.

She trembled under the pressure of his fingers. He was hot against hers, pressing against her with a need which she experienced in equal measure. He didn't wait for an answer —perhaps he didn't even need one, her body gave full answer anyway—but captured her lips with his own once more. Her arms snaked up around his neck and she pushed her fingers through his hair, so strong and thick. He pulled away. Their foreheads met, their chests heaving and pounding against each other, their mouths breathless with want.

"Then take me, Luca."

He didn't need telling twice and his mouth descended to hers—hot and searching—and his hands slid up and around her, holding her possessively and close.

She was drowning in sensation. There was nothing except Luca. The thud of his heart, felt and heard through her body, was as fundamental and powerful to her as the dull roar of the sea, like the blood in her ears. And the feel of his lips and hands upon her, was as essential as the air upon her skin.

But suddenly he pulled away. She curled her hand around his neck and tried to bring his head back to hers once more. But she felt only the curve of his lips as they formed a smile against her lips before he withdrew again.

"But I can't. Not here. We have no protection."

Their lips met again in a brief kiss before he took her hand and pulled her after him.

They ran along the darkening beach. It was empty and the long twilight cast a veil over reality. She was barely aware of her surroundings: only conscious of her struggle to find a firm footing in the soft sand so she could run faster, driven by the urgent demands of her body. He stopped at the foot of the wooden steps that led up to the house and kissed her—a deep, breathless kiss. Then they ran up the steps and through the open doors, a stream of sand following them onto the pristine surface.

He pulled her into the master suite and stopped suddenly, turning her round to face him, tilting her face to the light and then pressing his lips to hers.

His hands drew up her bare legs, cupping her bottom and drawing her to him. He was hard against her and she pushed aside his shirt with frantic hands as her need to touch his skin grew uncontrollable. His muscles flexed under her touch and she was aware of his quickened heartbeat as his fingers pushed up inside her panties, until his hands gripped her bare flesh and the taut fabric increased the pressure against flesh that throbbed with need.

She responded instinctively to the latent strength of his body—which was held back, restrained—and kissed his heated skin, breathing him in deeply and reveling in her power as she felt the effect of her mouth on him: his breathing coming shorter, his body trembling with suppressed desire.

As his hands pushed her panties down, she tried to undo the last remaining button on his shirt but her fingers, clumsy with need, fumbled and it wouldn't budge. The frustrations of years culminated in a spike of passionate anger as she tore the shirt open, leaving the obstinate button still attached, but his taut, smoothly muscled stomach available to her trembling hands and mouth. She sank against his chest and pressed her mouth to his skin, tasting, kissing, inhaling him.

"Turn around." His voice was gruff and in command and she knew that the restrained power she'd felt, was surfacing.

She stepped back unsteadily and he caught her and turned her around. Everything was heightened: her body was tense with need for him, jumpy to every touch but she had no option but to do what he said. His hands were too strong and their mutual need, too great.

She shivered as he pushed her hair away and slid down the side zip. She arched back against him as he slipped his hand inside her dress. Her stomach jumped under his touch and throbbed with a deep, intensifying need as he nuzzled the side of her neck. His hand then slipped lower, one finger barely touching where she needed to be touched. She pushed back farther, standing on her toes to allow him access to the place where all her sensations coalesced. But he didn't touch her there.

Instead, he withdrew his hands and swept down her dress until it lay pooled around her ankles. She stepped out of it, her heart beating twice as fast now she stood apart from him, their bodies not touching. She could feel his control. But she didn't want his control. She pressed back against his chest and felt the hardness of his erection pressing against her soft skin. She wriggled lightly against him.

"First things first, contessa. The rest, as beautiful as it is, has to go." She reached around to unclasp her necklace but he halted her hand with his. "Keep the pearls on, they are a part of you. But this—no." He traced his finger over the top of her breasts where the line of lace began before unclipping her bra from behind.

The bra fell to the floor and he turned her in his arms. His eyes were dark with desire as his hands took hold of her breasts, cupping them before describing one firm circular movement with his thumbs that tugged and tightened her need within.

She tried to draw him close but his hands slipped under her and he picked her up and carried her to the bed. He lay her down and knelt above her.

"Let me look at you."

He took hold of her hands and kissed her closed knuckles, each one, tight white in the moonlight and stretched them out behind her head. The movement shifted her bare breast and her nipple grew harder as his eyes and breath lingered on it. Involuntarily, she moved her breast closer to his mouth but he didn't take it immediately. She couldn't tell his thoughts in the semi-dark, guarded by the shadows and by his hair that fell over his face, showing only lips that parted slowly as he came closer, breathing her in, making her flesh goose-bump under his breath.

Then, when she thought she could bear it no longer, he dipped his head and kissed her soft flesh on all four sides surrounding the nipple that moved under his mouth. It bent toward his lips as he moved across to the other side. She thrust her hands in his hair and tried to pull him onto her more fully but he resisted, slowly dipping his head and flicking his tongue over her nipple. But as her hands roamed his body she knew that he couldn't resist her for much longer. As her fingers found his tip, his whole mouth fell over her nipple and he suckled hard. She jerked her head back and moaned as the spiraling intensified inside. She shifted her legs to accommodate his weight wanting that weight, now more than ever, between her legs.

He eased himself back, pushing harder onto her hips and watched the rise and fall of her breasts before he dipped his head and suckled both breasts, one after the other—hard—and she cried out, unable to hold on any longer.

Then he moved down: his tongue exploring the curves and valleys of her body, stopping at the scar that was the site of her injury. He reached down and kissed her scar, breathing her in as he did so.

"I wish I'd known years ago about this. I'd have kissed the pain away."

"Some scars go deeper."

"Then I shall kiss those away too." He caught her lips with his own and made sure that no more words were uttered, that there was no mention of any more scars, any more pain, only pleasure.

Isabella had forgotten how his lips could rob her of her thoughts, and break down the separation between their bodies, until there was only one feeling, only one sensation they both shared. But, like seven years before, kissing wasn't enough.

He stood up and deftly removed the trousers that she'd half undone. He opened a packet and swiftly rolled on a condom and returned to her. He knelt back on the bed and drew his hands up under her hips and kissed her intimately, his tongue teasing and tasting until she could stand it no longer and pulled him up to face her.

He hesitated, his eyes searching her face before he kissed her. She held his head in her hands, urging him for contact as her legs slid up the sides of his and wrapped around him, drawing him into her, slowly so slowly that she gasped with each exquisite movement inside her. How could she have forgotten such bliss? He filled her so completely in every way.

Once inside her he held himself there, looking down at her, as if unable to move. But she couldn't hold on and came suddenly just at him being inside her, at the tensions in and around her body, so subtly stimulated. She trembled and pulsed around him and she saw the effect of her body on him, as he started to move in her, pulling away before pushing deeply once more. His rhythm slowly increased and, as it did, her own sensations began to spiral out of control once more until he held her and thrust, short, sharp thrusts deep inside her and she clung to him, her lips finding his neck and tasting him there, before they both came in an explosive climax and they held themselves, tense, close for a brief moment, before falling back against the bed, sated.

LUCA GATHERED her in his arms and rolled onto his side, holding her tight against him, still inside her, feeling her still trembling body all around him. He kissed her face, his hold on her fiercely possessive. "Why has it never been like this with anyone else, Isabella?"

She shook her head as she nestled into his neck. "I can't answer that, Luca, because I've never been with anyone else."

"In seven years?"

There was a part of him that was pleased: a possessive, very male part. She was still his—his Isabella, still his. He felt himself harden at the thought and touch of her and he thrust deep inside her and watched her respond: her eyes closed, eyelids fluttering, and swollen lips parted. He held himself there, waiting for a long moment. Then her hips rose to meet his in invitation and he pulled out slowly, so slowly until only the tip of him was within her lips and then he sunk down into her delicious depth once more and lost himself in forgotten pleasure.

THE PALE LIGHT of a new day crept in so slowly that Isabella was barely aware that the day was dawning until Luca's fingers' softly trailed down her side, outlining the curve of her breast and the peak of her nipple as it responded to his touch. She turned to look at him, her breast conveniently falling into his hand as she did so.

"So it wasn't a dream. You're still here."

"I'm not going anywhere, cara."

"I was dreaming of the first time we made love. Do you remember?"

"Of course. I couldn't believe that such a quiet girl had such a depth of passion."

"And I couldn't believe that a man could be so gentle, so loving. But it was afterwards. I felt then, what I feel now. Just right. Content. We lay under your coat as the night air made me chill."

"And listened to your father walk up to your door, try the handle and then leave."

She withdrew her hand but he captured it in his own again. "I'd never been so scared."

"I had no idea. If I had, I would have—"

She pressed her fingers to his lips. "Don't talk of him. Tell me about you. You never did tell me what made you take the job at the castello."

He squeezed her hand and lay back, his eyes turned to the pure white ceiling along which shadows flickered.

"The only reason I took the job at the castello was to get back at my father. He hated the fact that grandmother worked there and getting a job there seemed the best way to show him that I wanted nothing to do with him." His hand stroked hers in a rhythm she sensed was automatic as his mind strayed back in time.

"Why did you bother? Surely he'd never have known?" Isabella frowned.

"He wanted me back in his life when he discovered I'd be his only son."

"And so you chose to work at the castello rather than to work in your father's business?"

"Yes. That about sums it up. I returned home after University." He grinned. "A great disappointment to my father."

Isabella rolled over and put her arms around him, resting her cheek on his chest. "I'm so sorry, Luca. Sorry for that little boy, needing so much and receiving only rejection from the very people who should have given him everything."

He lay very still for a long time and she watched as his expression became thoughtful, a slight frown pressing down upon his eyes, shadowing them, as if re-playing her words over in his mind. Then the frown lifted and he smiled and slowly trailed his hand down the side of her body, in at the waist before resting on the curves of her bottom.

"You know. Growing up I thought I would never have children. I never wanted to inflict on them what my father had inflicted on me. But when your mother told me you'd aborted our child, I was devastated. Believing you'd got rid our child changed everything for me, in so many ways that you have no comprehension of."

"Try me."

His fingers traced some unknown pattern on her skin as if he were trying to work out a solution to a puzzle.

"You know, of course, that I was married"

"Yes. Your grandmother told me. Not happily."

"Indeed. Not happily. It turns out she wanted money more than me." He smiled ruefully. "And I ignored all the signs. You know why?" He suddenly held her gaze and Isabella froze. "Because she was pregnant and refused to even contemplate getting rid of the child. I wanted someone like that: someone who wanted me, who would commit to me. Who would accept our child into her life."

"But, you have no child. What happened?"

He held her gaze now, keeping her hands tight within his own.

"I *do* have a child, Isabella. I *do.* Her name is Allegra."

Isabella rolled onto her back and tried to pull her hands from his but he wouldn't let them go. Angry now, she yanked her hands away and rose from the bed, plucking a gown from the back of the chair and wrapping it firmly around her body. She pushed her hair off her face, looking every which way but at him as the anger mounted. Only then did she turn to him.

"Why didn't you tell me, Luca? Why?" Her voice trembled on the last word.

"For obvious reasons. You were out of my life and she was all my life was about. And now that we are close once more. Now that it's time to tell you, I have."

Isabella felt cold and sick. "You have a child? And you accused me of keeping the truth from you?"

"She is *my* child, mine and my ex-wife's. Isabella, cara, why do you think I should have told you? Secrets remember, are only secrets to people involved. There was no reason to tell you before now."

"Yes, you should have because..." She shook her head, unable to state why he should tell her something that felt so incredibly personal to her, but that, of course, wasn't connected to her in the least. Until now.

"I'm re-thinking the castello."

She jerked her head to look at him again, confused at the apparent change of subject. "The castello? What? Why?"

"I still want it for a family home. But I want it for me, for Allegra, for you, for our future children. I want a big family, Isabella. And I want you. It's all I want now."

Suddenly the wide scope of her future—as wide and as unfathomable as the Atlantic—had just closed in on itself. Even if she could come to terms with the fact that Luca had a child, it was impossible. What he wanted from her was impossible. She'd meant it when she'd referred to her scars as not being superficial. The broken tissue traveled deep within her body, damaging her organs, her tubes, her hope of ever having another child.

CHAPTER 10

"*D*on't do this."

But his plea hung in the air between them, not reaching her. He watched her retreat before his eyes.

First her eyes: like a shutter drawn down silently, a veil fell across their grey depths. Then her arms: pulled into her body, her shoulders stiff as she turned away from him and finally her hands automatically smoothing her hair from her face, twisting its loose length into an unbound ponytail before hesitating when she realized she had nothing to bind it and helplessly letting it fall down her back in a twisted skein.

"Don't do this, Isabella."

But she didn't look at him. She started to walk to the window, her face silvered on one side by the light, but he caught her hand, insisting she stay but she didn't turn around. Simply stood, one hand helplessly held by his.

"You're leaving me already, Isabella. Don't do this again. You must tell me what you're thinking."

She shook her head, pulled her hand from his loose grasp and moved away. He rested his forearms on his legs and looked down at the wooden floor briefly, trying to work out what the hell he could do to make things right again.

"You *know* why I didn't tell you about Allegra."

"But I don't know why your grandmother didn't."

"Because I didn't wish her to."

"And so she never saw her?"

"Yes of course she did. She came to visit at our home in Como and the US."

"Of course."

"I know it's a surprise, but I *have* a past. I have seven years when you weren't around."

"I know that."

"It's more than that, isn't it? Tell me, Isabella."

She cleared her throat. "There's nothing to tell. You want a family home I'll make sure you have one."

"That's only half of it. What about the other half? What about being with me."

He stood up and walked behind her, his eyes taking in every inch of her hair, her body, its slight tremor, the tension in the shoulders.

"We came here to get away from the past. Leave it at that, Luca."

"We're not talking about the past now. We're talking about the future."

"Not now."

There were a million things he could say, a million things he wanted to do to slam through her evasiveness. He reached over to her but there was something in the way she turned her head slightly that made him stop. The early sun caught her cheekbones, casting her face in shadow: a shadow that was also present under her lashes and under the line of her jaw, a shadow that he felt, now, he'd never remove. He wanted to physically tear at it, destroy the shadow from her that refused to leave. He could do anything, he *had* done everything, except have the one thing he wanted more than any other.

"OK." He shifted away from her, his frustration increasing as he watched her relax. She hated confrontation. He knew that was the way with her. Nothing he could say or do would bring her round. She had to do that on her own. But he wasn't going to give her up without a fight.

"Why don't you go and get ready? We're due in New York shortly."

"I have meetings booked, but not till later. What do you have planned?"

"I'm meeting Allegra off the plane from Australia. And, cara, I would very much like it if you were there too."

She shook her head.

He felt the anger mount inside him. His daughter, his lover. He wanted them to meet; he wanted them together. "Why not?"

"I have meetings planned. What about them? What about work? And there are the art galleries, the Museum of Modern Art, meetings with architects and designers I've booked."

He curled his fingers into his palms, the nails biting into his flesh. He had to be calm. "Unbook them."

"That would be unprofessional."

"Isabella!" There was a world of frustration in his exclamation. A world of hope exploded, of future, fragmenting. He took a deep, shuddering breath. He had to make her see how important this was to him. "It's my daughter we're talking about. I want you to meet her."

"Well I don't."

"I see." And he did. The look of her, chin tilted up obstinately, eyes glittering with defiance, took him directly back to meeting his stepmother for the first time. He'd been Allegra's age. He'd been as vulnerable as Allegra. He wouldn't let what happened to him, happen to Allegra.

"Right. You need time. I understand." He looked up into eyes that doubted him. He nodded his head. "I do understand. But I also need you to understand something. Allegra will be coming back here this evening and you will meet her. And when you do, you must not hurt my daughter. She," he turned away briefly, trying to contain his pain, "she must not be hurt." His heart was pounding with anger so that he could hardly speak and also something he was not used to feeling— fear. He looked up at the ceiling and took in a deep, jagged breath. Then he looked at her again. "You wondered, once, where I was vulnerable. You've found it."

He turned to leave.

"Where are you going now?"

"Asking out of curiosity?"

She nodded.

"To shower, to dress and then to the zoo, cara. Nothing underhand, nothing designed to make you uncomfortable. The zoo." He hesitated one more moment, glanced at her but saw an impenetrable wall. He'd had a chance and he'd let it slip through his fingers. "I'll see you back here later. I'll organize a car to take you where you need to go—where you prefer to go."

He slammed the door behind him and entered the guest suite. He flicked the shower on full and got under it before the icy blast warmed up. He hardly felt the cold water slam against his body, he was so angry.

He understood her confusion. She needed time. But his understanding didn't eclipse the fear he felt for his daughter. It was OK for Isabella to be mad with him. It was OK for Isabella to ignore him. But it wasn't OK for her to treat his daughter how he himself had been treated as a child. He'd never seen any similarities between Isabella and his stepmother before but they were as clear as daylight now: neither wanted anything to do with a kid that was not their own. The reasons might be different but the effect was the same and he wasn't having it with his child.

LUCA WATCHED as Allegra raced around the zoo in a hyper state of jet lag. He willed himself not to run to her, not to pick her up in his arms and hold her close. And he didn't. That wouldn't help her. But he could watch over her.

While his ex wife had disappeared into her new life with her new husband apparently without a qualm, he didn't feel so easy about Allegra. Although he knew that the staff he'd hired to watch his daughter were second to none, while she was with him, he'd be there for her, watching her. The doctors had declared that she'd made a stunning recovery, but still. What if it happened again?

"Papa!" the girl slammed into his arms and he lifted her high in the sunshine, feeling his love for her flood his body.

He gave her a bear hug. "How are you feeling, carina?"

The girl grimaced at the question and wriggled away again. "Fine. Just wondered—"

Luca ruffled her hair looking into her eyes to see if she really was well. "What did you wonder? About the snakes? I know nothing other than the Riccioli's snakes of Italy that I used to roast on a fire."

"You ate them?"

Luca nodded. "Sort of. I pretended to eat them in front of my friends."

"Cool. No, what I was wondering is, who's that lady over there who's watching us."

Luca turned quickly to see Isabella standing in the shade of some trees trying to appear inconspicuous and failing.

Elegant and beautifully dressed as always, she looked as if she should be on a model shoot, not in the zoo.

He let Allegra slip down from his arms but wrapped one arm possessively around her shoulders. "That's my friend, Isabella."

ISABELLA HAD BEEN STRUGGLING to contain the confusion of feelings at the sight of Luca with the small girl but, as soon as he turned and caught her eye, she knew she no longer had the luxury of distance. She began walking toward them, her courage strengthening with each step until the girl looked up at her and smiled—Luca's smile. She stopped in her tracks.

She'd wondered how she'd feel when she met her. But, watching the small girl run and jump into Luca's arms, she congratulated herself. The hurt was still there, but it was numbed by the tight grip of her control. She felt its extent but not its sharp, probing pain. She smoothed the wrinkles out of her skirt.

She purposely didn't look at Luca as they approached to meet her half way, scared he'd undo her focus.

"Allegra, this is my friend Isabella. Isabella, Allegra."

Isabella extended her hand and noticed the brief look of confusion when the girl stopped both her arms from rising to accept a hug and instead thrust a hand forward. Allegra's hand was lost in hers as she gently squeezed it in greeting.

"Lovely to meet you, Allegra."

"And you, Signore Isabella."

Her accent was a gentle Australian-American blend. Isabella felt a rush of warmth that she instinctively countered with fear and stepped back abruptly. Embarrassed at such a public display of her private confusion she looked at Luca. He'd noticed but had stepped toward his daughter and swept her in his arms so that, even if Allegra had wondered at her abruptness, it would have only been for a second before she was lost in the moment with Luca. From behind Luca, Isabella saw an expression of pure, wide joy fill Allegra's pale face.

Luca turned away from Isabella, still with Allegra in his arms and strode across the courtyard to look at an animal enclosure.

He didn't wait for Isabella who followed helplessly behind. He hadn't even bothered to ask her why she'd come when she hadn't wanted to. Didn't he guess she'd realized what a mistake she'd made? She'd been shattered by the revelation that Luca had a daughter. But she was Luca's daughter and Isabella wanted to meet her. She halted in the shadows surprised once more at how mature Allegra looked for her age. She'd assumed Allegra had been born some years after he'd left her and when she'd first seen her from a distance, she'd been struck by how much older she was than she'd imagined—until she'd got close and had been reassured. She was slight, couldn't have been more than five years of age. But her eyes held a maturity that puzzled. Some kids were like that, she supposed. She took a deep breath. She could do this, so long as she stayed removed.

THE ZOO WAS BAKING HOT. Isabella brushed back the stray hair that clung to her face and held onto the jacket that lay sweatily over her arm. Allegra, who seemed to have taken an obstinate interest in her, tugged her arm.

"And what's that?"

"An Asp Viper."

"Cool."

"Yes, indeed. They're cold blooded which means their body temperature adapts to whatever the surrounding temperature is." At last something she could talk about other than feelings.

Isabella knew Luca was watching her. She couldn't sense whether he was amused or still angry with her. Possibly both.

"That's very informative, Isabella. I had no idea you were such an authority on snakes."

They fell into step as Allegra ran to the next enclosure where her Nanny waited for her. "One remembers what one's interested in. I've always loved animals."

"And yet you have no pets." He stopped and stood directly in front of her. "Tell me, why is that? Why is it you block out anything you love from your life? Is it a habit or a deliberate defense mechanism—make sure nothing gets through to you?"

"You don't need to own something to have an appreciation of it."

He didn't move but Isabella stepped round him and walked over to Allegra who, this time, looked up at her with an eager smile.

"What's this?" Allegra wasn't even looking at the animal. Isabella knew she simply wanted to continue the connection she'd made with her. But she couldn't bridge the gap physically between them. Allegra represented everything she'd lost.

"It's a Snow Monkey from Japan. And you see the mother over there. She's the one in charge of them all—males included."

LUCA SAT BACK on the bench and watched them circumnavigate the monkey enclosure. She looked like a teacher, he thought absently. Suddenly Isabella looked up and caught Luca's eye and he felt the same shot of adrenalin he felt whenever he looked into her eyes, into her heart. That was why she averted them so often.

He wanted to stay angry with her. He didn't want her to reject Allegra or have any negative effect on his daughter. But he suddenly understood she was doing her best. Whatever was eating into her, she'd cut her appointments short and come to find them. She was trying to relate as best she could to Allegra.

He gestured for her to join him. She came and sat beside him on the bench.

"Perhaps I should go. I'm interrupting your time with Allegra."

They watched Allegra drop the wrapping of an ice-cream into the waste-bin. She'd obviously found something enthralling about the waste itself and she gazed intently into its dirty depths. They both smiled.

"I want you here and Allegra seems to be enjoying your company, despite your reserve, or perhaps because of it. My ex wife was too much the other way."

Isabella raised her eyebrows briefly. She hadn't imagined his ex wife like that. In fact she hadn't imagined her at all. She'd drawn a veil over his ex in her imagination.

"Bad luck you've gone from one extreme to the other."

"Si." He smiled.

They both laughed as Allegra tried to surreptitiously push her much-despised sunhat in the bin. Her nanny was beside her in a moment and retrieved it but before it could be placed back on her head the girl had flung herself on the ground, laughing and rolled down the grassy bank of the picnic area.

"She's like her father, too charming for her own good."

"My charm doesn't seem to work on you."

"You've no idea."

He shook his head. "No, where you're concerned I

haven't. I don't understand you. One minute you're so hot and engaged, the next an ice-queen. Stop living in the past, just stop it. Trust me and be with me—and with Allegra."

Isabella looked at the young girl whose blonde hair was now spiked with dried grass, the picture of happiness, of naturalness, of what might have been.

"I can't make you happy, Luca. I really can't."

"I think I should be the judge of that."

The tension was broken by the slapping sound of sandals on the hot path and a whoosh as the little girl landed on her father's lap, her feet kicking up in the air above Isabella's lap.

"Ready?' Luca looked across at Isabella who smiled.

"Ready." Isabella grabbed Allegra's feet while Luca slipped his hands under her arms and they took the wriggling, giggling girl to the top of the slope and rolled her down.

Isabella looked across at Luca smiling down at his daughter and felt the warmth that was in his eyes enter her, seep slowly into her veins, and flood through her body before she could stop it. But she discovered she didn't want to stop it this time.

IT WAS late and Allegra was tucked up in bed—snug and warm and content: her teddies in a row beside her, except for one, that was barely recognizable, scrunched in her hand.

"Thank you for showing me the animals."

Allegra's voice was sweet and persuasive but Isabella swallowed back the impulse to go to her. It was still too soon. She couldn't create unrealistic expectations for the child.

"It was my pleasure."

"Give Isabella a kiss goodnight, Allegra." Luca said from the doorway.

Allegra shook her head. "No. She doesn't want me to and

I don't mind. Other women are grabby, but she's not. She's nice."

Isabella squeezed the girl's hand, brought it up to her lips and kissed the back of her hand lightly. "Goodnight, princess."

The little girl pursed her lips in a parody of formal politeness. "'Night, contessa."

The last image of Allegra as they partially closed the door behind them was a contented wriggle and eyes closing under the soft glow of a nightlight.

The beach house with its pure, hard lines and austere beauty was now a home, filled with a child's paraphernalia. Luca slipped his arm around Isabella's shoulders as they walked past the wall of artworks and the floor to ceiling windows that overlooked the darkening ocean.

"You've a beautiful daughter."

"Umm, she looks like her mother."

Isabella swallowed the stab of jealousy. "No, I mean her nature. She's very sweet."

"That definitely doesn't sound like her mother."

She stopped and looked up at him. The dim light from the sitting room didn't reach the shadowy hallway and Luca was lit from behind by the moonlight reflected from the water. But she saw the tenderness in his eyes.

"No. It sounds like you." She reached her hand up and cupped his cheek. "You, Luca. You hide it behind that successful exterior: so decisive so strong but so—"

He held his finger to her lips. "I don't feel sweet now, Isabella." His voice was husky.

"What then?"

He laughed. "My daughter might like non-grabby women, but I appreciate a bit of 'grabbiness'. Don't hold back with me, will you?"

She laughed, a laugh that dissolved into a soft moan as his

hands reached around and pull her to him. They'd been heading for the sitting room but somehow he'd guided her into the master suite, bringing her body tight to his and kicking the door softly shut after him.

"I have to hold back, Luca. I don't want you believing I can give you more than I can."

"You are all I want."

His kiss stopped her shaking her head and left her limbs trembling. Too soon, they pulled away and reality hit her once more.

"You know that's not true. You want a future—a large family, the works."

"I just want now. I just want you. Forget the rest."

And under the spell of his lips, she did.

MUCH LATER THE house lay quiet. The only sounds were the constant rush and drag of the sea on the sand and the breeze snapping and curling the long fall of white curtains. Isabella shifted a little, pulling her arm away from his grip. He tensed his fingers.

"Trying to run away already?"

She didn't answer. He propped himself up on one arm while he traced his finger around her bare breast. She closed her eyes as her breast tightened with pleasure. Then he dipped his head and kissed her extended nipple. He groaned and was about to dip his head again when she stopped him: her hands framing his face, curving around the strong cheekbones and jaw.

He rolled on top of her, pushing his hands up either side of her shoulders while pressing his hips to hers. She wanted to respond but didn't move. "We need to talk."

"I don't. But if you feel the need, talk away."

She licked her lips and frowned, trying to concentrate as

he moved down, his lips seeking out the places that sent the most exquisite sensations skittering through her body.

"It's about what you want."

"I know what I want." He descended lower.

"No, really, the future."

"I can see the immediate future, what else do I need to know?" He immediately dealt a swift, hard lick to her clitoris that made her gasp and her insides quiver in anticipation. She inhaled a shaky breath as her hands sought his head. She had to stop him. She couldn't focus. But, instead her hands somehow wove through the curls of his hair, luxuriating in its silkiness as she sunk under the wicked torment of his mouth. His hands slid under her and drew her up to him until all coherent thought fled as her breathing grew impossible under the incessant sensory overload of his mouth upon her. A bolt of pure liquid energy shot through her as she climaxed and all thought was truly forgotten as she sat up and brought his body into hers, wrapping her legs tight around him, as if desperate for more, as if desperate to re-create the all-encompassing sensory overload that was the only way of quieting her thoughts, of consuming her guilt. That connection was everything.

CHAPTER 11

*I*t was everything. But it was still not enough to give them a future together.

As they lay side by side in the cool of the early dawn, the knowledge that they needed to separate engulfed her once more. He would go when he knew she couldn't bring him the future he wanted. And then she'd have nothing.

"OK, tell me now."

She hadn't even known he was awake. He lay perfectly still looking out at the sky, following the clouds as they moved high overhead. The light in his eyes changed as the clouds passed between him and the sun, creating shadows where none were before.

She opened her mouth to speak but it was dry, parched. She swallowed. Instead the moisture came from her eyes. She brought up an arm to hide her tears, to protect herself, casually pushing the back of her hand away until it lay across her forehead.

"I can't have children."

At that moment Isabella felt the full force of an emotional silence that was more deafening than any sound. She cleared her throat, thoughts tumbling through her head, swiftly replaced as new ones took their place. But only one remained. He didn't want her now. She cleared her throat.

"No children," he repeated quietly.

"No, I can't. The accident…it's impossible now." She cleared her throat again and pushed the back of her hand over her eyes again. "But that's OK, I've my sisters I need to look after, I've my work."

"Of course. Your responsibilities."

"Yes," she said quietly. 'My responsibilities." She pretended to rub her forehead with the heel of her hand and looked away from him, out the window. The clouds that spun quickly by were rimmed with a silver light that, despite its subtlety, upstaged the glittering sunlight on the ocean.

Still no response. She glanced at him from under her arm, which lay protectively over her face. He hadn't even blinked, not stirred at all. She took a deep breath and only just stopped the sob from rising up into her voice. "I'm so sorry, Luca, I didn't mean for us to re-kindle things, I didn't mean for you to believe you had a future with me. I'm so sorry…"

"You're sorry?" His voice was quiet and even but she sensed the tension in it.

"I tried to tell you I couldn't give you what you wanted, that this wasn't going to go anywhere, I tried to…"

He rolled over suddenly and she was overwhelmed by his naked body pressing against hers, its power and potency. He placed his hand over her mouth and she gasped against his warm palm.

"Stop, Isabella. Just stop saying 'sorry'. I don't want to ever hear you say that word again." She shook her head as her breathing quickened. He pulled his hand away as suddenly as he'd placed it upon hers and, instead, tapped his index finger once upon her lips. "Don't." Tapped again. "Don't say anything more." She shook her head again and he fell back.

"You want me to go." She knew it and didn't phrase it as a question.

He turned his head to her and she couldn't recognize, couldn't place the look in his eyes. He seemed both hurt and angry at the same time. But it was the power that conveyed both feelings that hit her.

"No, I don't want you to go."

"Did you understand what I said?"

"Of course. You can say it in English if you wish, I will still understand. My comprehension is not in question here. It's yours. It's *you* who do not understand." He pulled her to him, whispering fiercely in her hair. "Cara, it's *you* I want. Why can't you understand this? It's *you*. Why can't you believe this? Why?"

He dragged her arm from her forehead and pulled her face roughly to his. The shadows were no longer in his eyes; they were clear and certain.

"You don't have to answer because I know. You can't believe because you don't trust. But you will."

ISABELLA LOOKED DOWN across the sea of clouds that blanketed the Atlantic, and up to the heavy sprinkling of stars. The day would be extremely short as they moved across the time zones. And that was good because today was a day that always reminded her of what she'd lost.

August 28. It was to have been the due date of her baby—her baby's birthday. Instead it was a reminder of what might have been and what could never be. What others had—what Luca had—was barred to her.

"And what thoughts are making you look so wistful?'

She looked across at Luca who was meant to be working. But, instead, he was watching her, a puzzled frown on his face.

"Did I relinquish my privacy when I agreed to take on this contract?"

"Absolutely." The frown stayed but his hot gaze swept her body leaving her in no doubt as to his thoughts. He pushed the laptop away and leaned forward, his knees purposely brushing hers. "You have no privacy whatsoever."

"You are very bad." She failed to keep her face straight as he leaned across and deftly undid the top button of her shirt revealing the swell of her breasts above the bra. He sat back again.

"That's better."

"May I remind you that your daughter is just the other side of that door?"

"No, you don't need to. You're still decent, just indecent enough to stir my own imagination. But she's asleep at present. And besides, if she came in and saw me kissing you—"

"It wouldn't be the first time?"

"Yes, it would. But I doubt it would scar her for life."

"Perhaps I don't wish to be kissed."

"Perhaps, but I think you do."

"What makes you doubt my word?"

"Your bright eyes, the way you've licked your lips, making them moist and inviting."

"Perhaps I always look like that."

"You'd better not. I only want you to look like that for me from now on."

"The contract will be completed soon."

"But I have a proposal. A new contract."

She shook her head. "Luca. Be serious."

"I've never been more serious. You know what I want, Isabella. I want you with me, always. I want you to marry me. Will you?"

The dull roar of the jet filled the long silence between them. She looked away first. But he reached out and pulled her face to his once more. "Don't turn away."

"You want more than I can give you."

"Why do you consider you know better than me what it is I want?"

"Because you've told me you want a big family. And you know I can't give you one."

"OK. A big family would have been ideal. But I'm enough of a realist to know that not everything in this world is ideal. But you are. It's you I want. It's not so much a big family I want, as a loving one. And I can't have that with anyone else but you. Will you marry me, Isabella?"

All her defenses were shot. There was no retreating from this. She couldn't have said if the noise that came from her throat was a sob or a laugh—perhaps both—but whatever it was, was swept away by his lips as he moved forward and stole the words from her mouth.

By the time he sat back, she knew that no matter her doubts and fears she had to be with this man. Before she knew it he was slipping a ring—a big beautiful diamond ring —onto her finger.

"You were very sure."

"Yes, I was. And I am. And I hope you are too."

She twisted the ring and watched as it sparkled in the light.

She knew he loved her and she felt an overwhelming love for him. But what would happen as the years passed by? Would he resent her? She quashed her doubts. What was the point in doubting him when he'd made it clear that he wouldn't; that it was her he wanted. She had to trust him. She *did* trust him.

She reached over and kissed him, very gently, very softly on the lips. "I love you, Luca."

"And I love you, Isabella." He held her face in his hands, shook his head and grunted in frustration. "Contessa, have you any idea how much I want you?"

She grinned. "Yes, I have, as it happens."

"With Allegra next door, tucked up asleep and likely to wake any moment, we don't have the privacy I need to make real my day dreams."

"You could lock the door."

He laughed. "I could. But I won't, not for my daughter. I won't have her wanting to reach me and finding she can't." His face became serious, the grin gone. "Ever."

If she'd changed because of her past she suddenly understood that he couldn't escape his past either. He would always make sure his child received the love from her parents that had eluded him. She believed him when he said it was a loving family he wanted more than a large one. He demonstrated that love with Allegra every second he was with her. He needed Allegra to know she could trust him because he knew what it was like to live without trust. And so did she.

As if summoned by their talk, Allegra burst through the door and landed on the seat next to Luca, scrambling up into his arms. Kneeling on his legs, she looked out the window with wide eyes at the stars.

"They're different to the stars at home."

"How clever of you to notice."

Luca's eyes were warm with love as he loosely put his arm around Allegra's waist to steady her as she craned her neck to look out the window. He brushed her hair back and looked out with her. Their faces were in silhouette: Allegra's in front of his; his, slightly closer to the window. They both had the same charm, capacity for happiness and ease of gesture and manner.

Allegra grinned cheekily, showing the gaps in her teeth

and looked up into her father's face. "I didn't notice. I was told."

"Well how good of you to be so honest then."

Isabella smiled. She doubted there was anything the girl could say her father wouldn't delight in. She watched as Allegra put her hands on Luca's cheeks and rubbed them. "You've got dimples like me." She proceeded to drill her fingers into said dimples while Luca puffed out his cheeks making the dimples disappear. But it didn't stop her.

"Do that again and I will have to punish you."

A shadow passed over her heart at the long-forgotten words. Allegra did it again, giggling and Luca picked her up, squealing and tickled her. Same words but entirely different outcome. This was Luca, not her father. Allegra and Luca were a team: so close despite the weeks apart. She wondered if she could ever be a part of their relationship. She shifted awkwardly around and looked out the window where a scattering of lights indicated they were passing over some European coastline.

She heard Luca set the girl down and sit back. "So tell me who told you about the stars."

"Mama's new husband did."

"Is that right?"

Isabella could tell from Luca's strained voice that he was trying not to sound possessive about Allegra, or suspicious.

"He's nice, Papa. He's very nice to me. I heard him tell Mama that it wasn't fair on me to go traveling while I was there. That was nice, don't you think?"

"It was thoughtful."

"And kind. He's nice to Mama too."

"I'm pleased. And were you sad when they left."

"A bit. But I was happy because I was coming to live with you from now on."

"But you will see Mama in your holidays."

"But Mama can come to see us, can she not?"

"Whatever you want, angelo mio."

It was obvious to Isabella where Allegra's real affections lay and it was equally obvious the pain Luca had felt at having been forced to leave his child for a few weeks while she was with her mother.

"I just want to be where you are Papa. I missed you."

"And me, you. But now look, your dinner is here. You must try to eat well to keep up your strength."

Allegra stabbed her fork into the lightly cooked vegetables and brought it to her mouth with evident distaste. She thoroughly chewed it, even though her eyes watered, with a doggedness Isabella had to admire. Then she swallowed and took another forkful.

Before she popped it into her mouth she noticed Isabella looking at her. "Vegetables, I hate them but I have to eat them for my own good, everyone says. I was sick."

Isabella looked quickly up at Luca.

"And Papa nearly missed Nonna's funeral because I was so sick. But I'm OK now but need to build up my strength. I'm smaller than other girls my age, you see."

"There were a few problems at Allegra's birth. She was born early." Luca shifted in his seat, uncharacteristically uncomfortable. "Come, Allegra, buckle up, we're coming in to land."

Isabella put on her own safety belt. As she watched Luca attend to his daughter his words played around her mind, niggling at an earlier thought she'd had, refusing to go away.

The plane touched down and the roar of the reverse thrust filled the cabin. The roar continued in Isabella's head. "Tell me, Allegra, when is your birthday?"

She didn't look at Luca though she knew he was watching her; she could feel his eyes burning in to her, could sense the tension.

"15 September. Mama said that it should have been 1 October."

Isabella felt sick but she had to continue, she had to know. "And you will be…"

"Six, I'll be six."

The silence was as intrusive as the plane's roar. It seemed interminable but couldn't have been—Allegra only had time to swallow a mouthful before looking up at her.

Isabella took a deep, steadying breath. "Then you must have a very special present." She sat back, pushing the anger and betrayal back to that secret place inside for the moment. She mustn't let Allegra see.

"What? What will you get me?"

"Allegra," Luca interjected. "It's rude to pester."

Isabella turned to Luca and he recoiled under her cold glare. "She's not pestering. I would have done the same. Before I go," she swallowed and turned to Allegra, "I'll bring you a surprise."

"You're going somewhere?"

Isabella nodded, feeling Luca's eyes boring into her, willing her to look up at him. But she refused. Grief lay heavy in the pit of her stomach, waiting for the moment she could think about it. But, for now, she kept it low, kept it out of her head, kept it at bay. That way she could function. That way she could give the girl the attention she deserved.

"I've nearly completed my work and I've family in Florence I live with." The only pain Isabella felt was the pain of the girl's disappointment. The other, deeper grief was too vivid to contemplate.

"That's a shame, isn't it Papa. I thought Isabella was going to live with us."

Isabella couldn't help but smile at Allegra's adult polite turn of phrase: a smile that froze as she became aware of Luca shifting Allegra toward her Nanny.

"Allegra, go with Nanny and gather your things together."

"Sure, Papa." She leaned over to give him a big kiss on the cheek but for once she wasn't the focus of Papa's attention and he turned late and gave her an abstracted smile.

As the door closed he leaned over and took Isabella's hand but she pulled it away and looked at the ring that now seemed to represent all that was wrong with their relationship, a parody of what should have been. She pulled it off and tossed it at him. He caught it with one hand, held it tight in his fist.

"Isabella. Speak to me."

"And what would you like me to speak of? Hey? Perhaps trust? You told me you wanted me to trust you. That's laughable. How long did you wait after leaving my bed to have unprotected sex with Allegra's mother? Would you like me to ask you that?"

"It was weeks only. You know that. No doubt you've done the math."

To hear it from his own mouth made her gasp with the pain that refused to be kept at bay any longer. She shook her head, willing the tears not to appear. "How could you, Luca?"

"Don't—"

"Papa!" Luca turned to his daughter, the exasperated look giving way as he forced a smile to greet her.

"Excuse me." Isabella rose and went to the bathroom and sat, head in hands, wondering what the hell she was doing there and how the hell she was going to get out. Because get out she would. Luca had forced her to believe in him again: had made her vulnerable, had made her trust him when all the time he'd been creating a big bald lie about himself. He'd betrayed her.

She splashed water onto her face and looked up into the mirror. Her face was white, her hands shaking. How could she trust him again?

They were waiting by the open door: Allegra filling the silence with her chatter while Luca stared at Isabella, willing her to look at him, willing her to understand the incomprehensible. She shook her head, as if to herself, but knowing that he would realize the message was for him. There was no getting around this.

How could she trust in someone when the proof of his infidelity was holding Luca's hand tight: happy and enchanting and blissfully unaware of the maelstrom she'd unwittingly created?

WITH NOWHERE ELSE TO GO, somehow Isabella had managed to remain calm and controlled for Allegra's sake. But, as they reached the castello, the control began to crack. But there was no retreating with a child around. Once outside in the ancient cobbled courtyard, Allegra grabbed Isabella's hand on one side and Luca's on the other and demanded a swing as they walked to the double doors of the castello.

"It's soooo cooool, Papa. It's like something out of the history books. It doesn't seem real."

Luca cleared his throat as if trying to focus on her words. "In Australia maybe, but not here. Here, such places are very real—they're everywhere."

The flatness of Luca's tone revealed his true thoughts. He was trying hard to be normal and responsive to Allegra. After all, none of this was her fault. And she was the daughter he'd always wanted and would never get from Isabella.

Allegra jumped up and down. "And I'm going to live here too." Then she remembered her manners and turned to Isabella. "And you have always lived here, contessa?"

"Yes. I was born here and lived here all my life."

"Then you would have enjoyed continuing to live here with us."

Isabella bit the inside of her lip, willing her mouth not to tremble. "It's time to move on." She sucked in a deep breath before she squeezed Allegra's hand. "Let's go inside and I'll show you around."

A wall, as solid as those now newly gleaming and repaired, had risen around Isabella's thoughts. They'd frozen as they'd sprung up in response to the realization that Luca had been unfaithful to her all those years ago. And she was grateful. It allowed her to talk about the castello, to act as the remote tour guide she'd become. It allowed her to function. She'd think and feel later.

At last they arrived outside the turret room. "Here, this is your room, Allegra. Your Papa insisted. He thought it would be perfect for you." She looked around at the room that had been refurbished according to his specifications in their absence. It looked beautiful. "It has always been a favorite of mine. I hope you enjoy it."

"This isn't like castles I read about in Australia."

"It's not?" Luca frowned.

"No, it's like a home."

Isabella turned quickly to walk away but hadn't antici-pated Allegra would fling her arms around her legs. Isabella closed her eyes and gently brought her arm around the girl's shoulder for a moment before her hand fell away.

"Thank you, Isabella, for giving me your favorite room. I'll look after it for you."

Isabella nodded and smiled tightly, willing the tears to remain unshed as she walked slowly out of the room and down the stone steps.

Allegra's voice drifted down to her from above. "Did I say something wrong Papa?"

"No, Allegra, you said something right."

Isabella stood on the balcony, looking across the dark valley down to the lights of the village. It was late and she couldn't sleep. The air shifted as her door opened and closed but she didn't turn around. She knew he'd come.

"You have a wonderful daughter, Luca."

"She's the best." His voice came to her from the dark room, disembodied. "I'd hoped you'd grow to love her."

"I'm sure I would have done. But we both know that's not going to happen now."

"I know nothing of the sort."

She turned round to see him emerge onto the balcony, so compelling, so much of what she wanted, and yet, now, so out of reach. The anger jumped up inside her and she shot out her hand and tried to slap him around the face. But his hand came up and caught hers before it made contact.

"Don't you dare blame me, Isabella. Don't you dare."

It was all she needed to let the wall crumble and release the pent-up emotions of frustration, of longing and of utter fury. He'd robbed her of her happiness with one stupid act.

"I dare." She pushed past him into the room. "I dare all right. Seven years ago, I lay in my room, dreaming of the time when we could be together. Discovering with joy that I was pregnant, while you," the tears had begun to stream down her face now, "while you, were busy making another woman pregnant within weeks." Her voice cracked at the word "weeks" and she turned away so he couldn't see her. A cry wrung its way from the depth of her body and she slammed the flat of her palm against the window, furious at this final betrayal. But he grabbed her shoulders and forced her to turn and look at him.

"All I knew was that you didn't want me. What the hell was I meant to do?"

"Of course, what am I thinking? It was the obvious reaction, go and make someone else pregnant."

"Your father told me to get out, *you* didn't want me, you made no attempt to respond to my calls."

"You *knew* how much I loved you. You *knew*."

"No. No, I didn't. Do you think telling me to go, then not speaking to me, not having anything to do with me was a sign of love. Hey? God damn it, Isabella, look at me. Stop retreating. You're slipping away from me again."

"No. I've slipped away. I've gone." She pulled away from him. "I trusted you, Luca, like I'd never trusted anyone else."

"Not enough to tell me about what really happened to our child. Not enough to tell me about your father."

"That wasn't about trust. That was about grief and guilt."

Suddenly his hands were on her shoulders. "I'm sorry, Isabella. But you need to understand—"

She slapped his hands away, turning to face him. "I understand perfectly. Within weeks of leaving my bed you were having sex with someone—anyone it sounds like. You cheated on me, Luca. You cheated on me…"

Her voice faded as she tried to turn away again.

"Come on, you weren't there. You stood by and watched your father threaten me, you stood by and accepted his ruling that I should leave. You watched me go. What should I think? You even told me to go, to leave you."

"It was only going to be for a while, until he'd calmed down. I was scared…"

"I wasn't into compromises then and I'm not now."

"Then tell me how it was."

"Why? Would it make any difference? Would it change things if I said I'd known my ex wife in Rome when I was at University? Would it change things if I said she couldn't get enough of me and I couldn't get enough of being wanted? God knows I'd had little enough of it growing up."

"And is that still what you want? Attention? Like some attention-seeking child?"

He turned away. "Of course not. I want you, you know that. I have my daughter and I want you. Is that too much to ask?"

She swallowed. "Yes, it is. I'll finish my work and leave."

"No. This time I'm not letting you go so easily. This time I'm going to see this out. And you will, too."

"Don't you understand Luca? What's to stop you doing it again if I do or say the wrong thing? I couldn't have entertained the possibility of making love with anyone other than you. Not at any time over the last seven years: especially not immediately after we parted. How could you?"

"We're different, you and I. You retreat into yourself when things aren't going well. But I don't like what I see in myself and I advance, toward others. I need them, I need their approval in a way you'll never understand. It's a weakness, I know. But it was there, for many years." He caught her hand firmly in his once more. "But that's gone now. Having Allegra taught me a lot about love. There's nothing I need from love, nothing I seek to gain from loving. Nothing I have to run away from any more. It won't happen again." He pulled her to him tightly and kissed the top of her head, pressing his cheek to her head, holding her more tightly as she tried to wriggle away from him. "I promise, it won't happen again. Ever. Don't do this Isabella. I need you."

She stopped still then and an uneasy calm fell over them both. "You don't need me. Don't kid yourself you do." But she continued to look at him, shaking her head in confusion, as she slipped her hand out of his. He let it fall. There was nothing more he could say.

"I'll leave."

"You've not finished your work."

"Surely you don't expect me to continue under such circumstances."

"The circumstances make it even more necessary for you to continue. You are to complete your work as planned. If you don't I'll sue you for breach of contract."

"You know I can't afford a legal fight."

"Of course I know. You *will* stay. You will *not* run away again."

"I'll do what's required of me, but no more."

She turned back to the window and it was only when the air shifted once more that she knew he'd left the room as quietly as he'd entered.

CHAPTER 12

*L*uca leaned back against the castello wall and watched Allegra jump into the pool, closely followed by half a dozen of the village children who'd arrived to help her celebrate her birthday. He wiped the splashed water from his face.

"Papa! The water pistols!"

He lobbed the pistols into the water and they were immediately pounced upon by the children. "No shooting water outside the pool!" He knew his words wouldn't be heeded and he didn't care. He could watch Allegra all day. Somehow, within the space of a few short weeks, she'd managed to become part of an inseparable gang of village kids and he'd never seen her so happy, nor so well. She was thriving. He sighed and leaned back against the wall once more. He wished he could say the same for himself.

He'd not sought out Isabella since their return from the US. What was the point? There was nothing he could say that hadn't already been said. He'd been stupid and he was paying the price. She had to realize he'd changed and he couldn't help her with that. It had to come from her. But time had just run out. She'd left word she'd be leaving today and there was nothing he could do to stop her.

At a shout from Allegra, he looked up to see Isabella step out of the castello into the bright sunshine. He frowned as he noticed the flat shoes, the wide-cut white trousers and the form-hugging strappy top. They were light years away from her usual tight skirts and high heels, but still incredibly stylish. He exhaled a breath he hadn't known he was holding. The change in style didn't mean a thing. He was grasping at straws. She hadn't changed and she wasn't going to. She'd made that quite clear.

"Look Papa! Isabella has a present for me!"

He watched as Isabella struggled to contain an unwieldy looking present before placing it on the ground. It was immediately surrounded by a group of dripping children. Allegra dropped to her haunches and began untying the pink ribbons that festooned the box. She stopped suddenly. "What's that?" She bent her ear to the box where there were a series of holes and listened and then jumped up and down excitedly. "It was a bark, I'm sure it was a bark!"

Luca laughed and Isabella looked up and caught his eye. Her direct gaze held his and he saw something he'd never before seen in her eyes: something direct and strong. Then she turned away. No, he must be imagining it. He couldn't put himself on the line any more just to be knocked back again. It was an unguarded glance—that was all. He fisted his hands in his pockets—trying to control the instinctive need to move close to her—and stayed where he was.

Allegra opened the box and a chocolate brown labrador puppy jumped out yapping furiously. Allegra chased it, picked it up and gave it a big hug.

"Thank you, Isabella. Thank you. I love her. It is a 'her', isn't it?" Allegra held up the puppy with an appraising eye as she checked it out and then turned back to Isabella with a cheeky grin. "Yeah, it is." She ran off with the labrador firmly clasped to her body, with the other children in hot pursuit.

Isabella was left alone: her white trousers sprayed with pool water from the kids and covered in dog hair from where the puppy had tried to climb her legs. But she didn't appear to have noticed; she watched Allegra with a smile that Luca couldn't take his eyes off. He recognized it. He pulled the small, dog-eared photograph from his pocket. It was of Isabella, aged ten, with the smile that he'd never seen—until now. He unclenched his fist and pushed himself from the wall and into the sunlight.

ISABELLA TURNED round to find Luca standing in front of her. A frisson of excitement sent her heart into overdrive. His expression was still cool, as it had been since their return to the US, but there was a wary interest in his eyes that was new.

She nodded. "Luca."

"You chose your present well."

She swallowed. "I thought she'd like her." A hundred thoughts ran through her mind and a hundred thoughts were dismissed. She had so many things to say to him: about her feelings and fears and she didn't know where to start, or even if he wanted her to. "The puppy's had her vaccinations so she's safe to run around."

"Looks like she was running around your trousers before you gave her to Allegra."

Absently, Isabella looked down and swiped at the brown hairs that clung to her white linen trousers. It had no effect. "Yes, she's hard to resist."

"You've never had any problems resisting the irresistible before."

She smiled. "And what exactly are you referring to?"

"People, maybe."

"*You*, maybe?"

He shrugged. "Now, Isabella, I would never admit to being so vain as to believe I'm irresistible."

"Then you've changed."

The small smile that quirked at the corner of his lips faded into a seriousness that was reflected in his eyes. "Yes, I have. And I can't seem to make you understand how much."

"I… I understand more than you realize."

"And is that enough?"

"For what?"

"To trust in me again?"

"Luca, I…" Her voice trailed off. How could she begin to explain the tide of feelings that had started as a slow trickle and that had become a torrent that threatened to overwhelm her fast-held beliefs? "You're the same man now, as you were seven years ago. I feel the same for you, I trust you the same."

Luca frowned and sighed. "Which means you don't trust me at all."

"No, I don't mean—"

Her words were interrupted by the loud toot of a car horn. Luca looked round and his eyes alighted on her packed suitcase in the doorway. He turned swiftly to her, his frown lowered over hurt eyes. "You're leaving."

She winced at the sudden coolness of his tone and looked down. "I've done my work here, you've kept your promise to Nonna. Time to move on." She looked up at him when he didn't reply. "Isn't it?"

"Yes, of course. You knew I wouldn't sue you. You've done a great job here. Everything is as it should be."

She nodded. How unemotional he sounded now. How resigned. Was it hurt or simply relief she was going away at last? She cleared her throat. "I'm sorry it's ended like this."

He shrugged. "It's probably for the best."

She frowned and the words she'd been framing, rehearsing, faded on her lips. "Luca, I—"

He held up his hand to stop her. "Let's leave it. I can't stand going over old ground any more."

"But—"

"No. You've made things very clear and I've come to terms with that. There's nothing more to be said." She ached to reach out to him but he obviously didn't feel the same.

The car tooted once more. "I'd better go."

He nodded without moving. "I'll explain to Allegra."

"She knows I'm leaving. I've already told her." She turned away and began walking to the taxi. Suddenly Allegra and her gang barreled around the corner and bumped into her. Allegra thrust the puppy into her arms. It was wriggling and she had no choice but to accept it. The puppy lifted its head to hers and licked her face. Allegra laughed loudly, as did Isabella, shocked out of the grief that filled her.

"She loves you! Just like we do." Allegra flung her arms around Isabella's legs. "But you're going now aren't you? I wish you weren't."

With one hand holding the wriggling, still licking puppy firmly, Isabella cupped the back of Allegra's head as she pressed against her hip. "So do I, Allegra, but I must."

"Why? Don't you love us?"

Isabella set the puppy down on the ground. "Yes, I do. I love you and your father very much, but sometimes that's not enough."

"It should be." Isabella jumped at Luca's voice so close behind her. She hadn't known he'd walked over to them. The dog had absorbed all her attention.

"Luca…"

"Allegra, take the puppy into the kitchen and get it some water. It's hot out here, it'll be thirsty."

"Sure, Papa." And Allegra and the other kids ran round the pool and into the shady castello.

"I thought I must have imagined the change in your smile earlier. But you've just done it again. I've only seen a smile like that once before."

Isabella was confused and shook her head. "Where? What are you talking about?"

Luca smiled. "It doesn't matter. I need to tell you that you can't go yet. There's something we need to discuss—something about the castello. There's a problem."

"What?"

"I'll show you."

"But, the taxi…" Then she turned and saw the taxi driver being given a large lemonade.

"I've told him to wait. Come on."

WHAT THE HELL was he talking about? A smile? A problem?

Isabella followed Luca into the castello wondering if he'd been out in the sun too long or if there really was a problem she'd not been told about. Either scenario made her anxious. When he stopped in the hallway, now filled with the scent of freshly picked flowers and beeswax, she studied his face for clues. It wasn't reassuring. His lips were quirked in a grin he didn't seem to be able to contain and his eyes darted restlessly around the hall. Then he appeared to make a decision and strode over to the main reception room. "I think we need to be in here."

She shrugged, completely bewildered, followed him into the room and looked around. It wasn't exactly as she'd planned but that was most definitely not her responsibility. The sunlight swept across the shining parquet floor from huge windows that overlooked the valley. Above them, the crystal chandelier sparkled and bounced a rainbow of colors over the newly cleaned stonework. In one corner she'd installed a subtle, comfortable arrangement of settees but, on the other side was a games area, including a full-size table-tennis table, she most definitely hadn't planned for. Isabella raised her eyebrows, bent down and picked up a bat that had dropped to the floor. She placed it carefully onto the table.

"Not exactly as I'd imagined it."

"No. Nor me."

"Well *you* added the table-tennis table. It doesn't exactly help the ambience."

She swung round to face him. His eyes searched hers as if looking for answers to a question she didn't know had been asked. She turned away abruptly, confused. She walked over to the window and threw it open, allowing a cooling breeze and the sound of the river into the room.

"Still seeking the soothing sound of the river? What will you do when you're away?"

She blinked. She hadn't even realized she was doing it. But he was right. She'd miss the sound of the water, flowing gently some times, raging at others, but always there, always soothing. "It's just habit. I'll miss the sound, I'll miss many things but I'll get by."

"What other things will you miss?"

"The castello, Allegra, you…"

"Me?"

She jumped at the proximity of his voice. She swallowed but didn't turn around.

"Yes, of course."

"You told Allegra you loved me. Did you mean what you said?"

"Yes."

"And I love you too."

"Not enough to be faithful though."

"I had no-one to be faithful to. You made sure of that." He sighed heavily and went to turn away.

Panic suddenly filled her. She touched his arm briefly and his hand went to the place she'd touched as if she'd burned him. "Luca, I know—"

"And if you can't see that what I did—while it might not have been the right thing to have done—was not about us at all but about my own inadequacies then…" He shook his head. "What did you say?"

"I know. I've gone over and over what happened. I'd thought the separation was temporary; you thought it permanent. What your father did to you made it too easy for you to believe I didn't love you enough."

He exhaled deeply and his shoulders relaxed with the release of tension. "Isabella, my only crime was to have been young and stupid and needing love more than anything in the world. It was *never* not loving you. *That*, I've always done —whether I've known it or not. We all make mistakes. I'm not the only one who has. Why can't you trust me?"

He held his mouth a kiss away from hers, his breath was hot against hers as she reached out for his hands.

"I've been trying to tell you, Luca. I *do* trust you. I was just so angry with you, so hurt, so upset. But, over the past few weeks, Luca, I've been thinking. I've changed so much, since you've come back into my life. Talking to you about the past, being with you, making love to you, it's made me strong in ways you can't imagine."

"Go on." He gripped her hands tightly.

"I *do* trust you. I always have. I trusted you the moment I first met you. Because of what happened, I—"

"Don't talk about that—"

"I just want to say that I was scared of men but when I met you I trusted you instinctively. And I was right. You've always been loving and kind. What you did, well, I understand. Of course I do. I can't say it doesn't hurt, because it does. But, more than that, I'm scared. I said I loved you but I don't know if I *can* love, if I can *feel*, like you do."

"There's only one way to find out. Stay with me. Be with me. Love me."

She shook her head. "Just imagine if I do stay and find there really *is* nothing inside me. You deserve more than the empty shell that's in here." She tapped her heart.

"I've learned to shake away my fears by not listening to them, not owning them, they've gone now when I look. They're not there. You should try it."

She began to shake her head in confusion but his hands reached out and held her head firm; his thumbs swept across her cheeks as if brushing away shadows.

"Just think how much you've changed in the last month. Just think how much further you can leave your past behind in a future we can share together. There's never any guarantees; all we can do is try." He kissed her gently and she knew she didn't stand a chance. "Stay?"

She nodded, her heart too full to speak. He kissed her again, except this time with a savage assurance that made all the doubts, all her own lingering insecurities and fears diminish beside the overwhelming love they shared.

Suddenly they were aware of shouts and the clawing sound of a puppy trying to change direction on a shiny parquet floor. Isabella winced at the sound and Luca pulled away. She turned and groaned at the sight of the scratch marks on the floor and the rumpled rug where the dog had finally gained traction.

"Papa, Isabella! What you are doing in here? There's a man outside who says he needs to leave. He sent me in to find you."

Luca turned to Isabella. "Well, Isabella?" He brought Isabella's hand to his lips and kissed it.

Allegra looked from one to the other. "Papa, you've that look in your eye. Like you have when you look at me." She turned to Isabella and, with a mischievous grin, echoed her father's tone and words, even if she didn't understand his full meaning. "Well, Isabella?"

Isabella laughed as she tried, without success, to stop the tears from falling. She looked away and brushed her eyes so she could see more clearly before turning back to them both. "Perhaps, Allegra, you could tell the cab driver I won't be needing him after all."

Allegra jumped and shot her fist into the air. "Yes!" She turned to Luca and exchanged a high five. "Result, Papa!"

Luca looked over Allegra's head at Isabella and gave her a look of such love that she knew she'd risk facing her worst fears to spend the rest of her life with someone she loved so much, someone she could see who loved her equally in return. She also knew that withstanding the seductive charms of one Vittori was difficult enough, but standing firm against two was completely impossible. "Result, Allegra!"

EPILOGUE

"*A*llegra! Bring the boys here!"

Isabella grinned as Gianni, so obedient to his beloved elder sister, immediately dropped the handful of river mud he was about to fling at Antonino and Antonino took advantage of his lapse in attention and hefted a handful of mud straight at Gianni's face.

The grin turned into laughter as she watched Allegra carefully remove the mud and then turn swiftly and land a handful of mud on Antonino who fell backwards into the shallow water laughing.

"You should be disciplining those boys, not laughing, Signora Vittori!" Luca's hands slid around her shoulders before he kissed her on the cheek.

"I don't need to with Allegra here. Gianni does everything she tells him and Allegra can sort out Antonino with a taste of his own medicine."

"The boys are so different, despite the same upbringing."

"I guess genes play a bigger part than I imagined. Different parents but we're lucky—both are wonderful, in different ways."

Luca took some bread from the picnic spread before them. It was cooler under the shelter of the trees and, as he closed his eyes, Isabella felt her throat constrict with happiness. "Tired?"

He flicked one eye open quizzically. "Not as tired as you must be, up most of the night with Dorotea."

Isabella looked down at the tiny baby, the result of many operations, now fast asleep, nestled close to her breast. "I think she's nocturnal, sleeps all day and up all night. Definitely genetic—takes after her father."

"Umm," Luca stroked her bare ankle, "her mother has also been known to stay awake all night making demands."

The reminder of their lovemaking sent a shiver of longing through her body, setting it alight with desire, before the flame curled around and settled in her heart. Isabella took a deep breath, savoring the happiness that had proved elusive for so many years. "I feel as if I've been so long asleep that I want to experience every moment now."

His grip tightened around her ankle, his eyes still closed, as he lay back under the dappled light. Despite the lack of sleep, he didn't look tired.

"It's lucky for you that I'm prepared to assist you in this exploration of experience." He sat up and leaned over and kissed her on the lips, his mouth lingering close to hers as his eyes searched her face. "If there are any experiences that you wish to have, just let me know. I'm prepared to do whatever I can to assist."

"Then kiss me again."

Suddenly running feet and muddy hands descended on them: the boys grabbed handfuls of food and flung themselves onto the picnic rug while Allegra stood bossily over them all, muddy hands on wet shorts.

"Papa, stop kissing Isabella! You'll wake the baby."

"Allegra, you look like a vagabond!"

Allegra looked down at her muddy and wet shorts and shirt and then back at him, an impish grin on her face. She jumped on top of him and gave him a big hug, soaking him with the cold river water. But one look at his mock-stern face and she leaped off, laughing, and ran to the river, with Luca hard on her heels.

The boys settled around Isabella, one stroking little Dorotea's dark downy hair and the other resting his head on Isabella's lap.

Isabella closed her eyes and listened to the shouts of laughter from Allegra and Luca, the tumbling of the water across the rocks and the birdsong overhead. Her fingers spread out searching for something and then rested when she found it.

The wildflowers, with their woody stems that clung to the rocks and crevices around the river, so tenacious, so intent on life, so reminiscent of Luca's grandmother. A strong woman could leave a legacy beyond death. Nonna had. And so would she.

The End

AFTERWORD

Dear Reader,

I hope you enjoyed Luca and Isabella's story. Reviews are always welcome—they help me, and they help prospective readers to decide if they'd enjoy the book.

The **Italian Lovers** series continues with book 3, *Trusting Him* (also published as *The Passionate Italian*), an excerpt of which follows.

If you enjoy reading about alpha heroes and the strong women they fall in love with, try my **Mackenzies** and **Desert Kings** series. The **Mackenzies** series is based in New Zealand and is about the Mackenzie brothers and their close friends. Then there's the **Desert Kings** and **Sheikhs of Havilah** series for those who like their romance on the more exotic side.

My newest series is **Lantern Bay** which follows on from the

Mackenzies. Find out more about all my books on my website—https://www.dianafraser.net/

You can sign up to my newsletter here if you'd like to be kept informed about new releases.

Happy reading!

Diana

After a year with Giovanni Visconti, Rose had disappeared, seemingly unable to deal with her husband's jealous and controlling nature.

Two years later Giovanni tracks Rose down, determined to prove he can be trusted. But Rose is keeping secrets from him—secrets that could destroy more than just their relationship...

Excerpt

..."So you don't want me to work. How exactly do you propose we spend the next twenty hours or so?"

He dropped his hand and she released her breath, not realizing she'd been holding it.

"I need to know you again."

His voice sent chills down her spine. There was an uncertainty evident in the rougher tone she'd never heard before. Her pulse raced at the implications of his words, their ambiguity, their potential.

"Why?"

He shook his head. "No more questions."

"It can't all be on your terms. Tell me. What do you need to know about me, that you don't already?"

His brow dipped into a brief frown, his dark eyes darkening even further as if a shadow had passed over them. "Consider it an interview—a prolonged interview. There are things I wish to know and which I will discover. We'll begin now but it won't end tonight."

"When then?"

"When I discover what I need to know."

"What the hell are you talking about?"

"It is my question I wish answered. Now get back into bed."

She shivered, confused and doubtful. "Ask me whatever it is. Let's get this over with."

"There's no rush." He moved to the phone and ordered some drinks. "We have all the time in the world."

She sat down before her legs gave way beneath her. "That time is gone, Giovanni, don't you understand? The time for talking, for listening, for understanding—it's gone."

"You refused to talk to me before, you gave us no time. Now, here's your chance."

"A chance I don't wish to take."

"You have no choice."

A discreet knock at the door was followed by the steward bringing in drinks and snacks. He laid them out on the coffee table and left without raising his eyes or talking. He was too well trained and well paid—too used to attending to his boss in a bedroom with sundry women—to make small talk, Rose supposed. Besides, the tension in the air was palpable.

"Drink?"

She shook her head. "One question then. Just one for tonight."

He laughed. "You've misunderstood. There will be no questions. I can get my answers without questions."

"You wouldn't!"

"I wouldn't what? Touch you?' He pushed the cover back off her. "Yes, Rose, I would."

"What can you hope to gain by violence?"

"Have I ever been violent with you?"

"No. Of course not—"

"Then I suggest it's unlikely I ever will be."

"Then what question are you trying to answer? Tell me that."

"A question that only your body can answer. Not your mind, not your voice, nothing else."

Heat simmered deep inside. She gasped at the intimation, the suggestion of what he was about to do to her.

"You wouldn't take me by force."

"You're not listening to me. I'm interested only in your body's responses to me, not in satisfying any physical needs of my own. No matter how pressing." He didn't smile, didn't move, simply held her gaze, watching, assessing, alert.

He put down the cup of untouched espresso and brushed her hand briefly with the palm of his hand. The gesture had a simplicity that took her breath away. Then he withdrew his hand, leaving her own hand sensitive, aware of the lingering warmth of his touch. He stood over her, watching, his gaze traveled the length of her, from the chest that, she knew, betrayed her increased heart rate and rapid breathing, to her jean-clad legs.

He walked away and flicked off the light, leaving on only the reading light beside the bed. Its light pooled on and around only her, leaving darkness and all its unknowable potential beyond her.

There was only this moment in time, with him and her. That sense of timelessness caught and held her, stemming the questions, the things she knew she should say, the things she knew she couldn't say. He was right. Her body held her in control now. And he was, had always been, master of that...

Buy Now!

ALSO BY DIANA FRASER

The Mackenzies

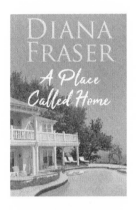

A Place Called Home

The View from Cliff House

Escape to Shelter Springs

What you See in the Stars

Second Chance at Whisper Creek

Summer at the Lakehouse Café

Lantern Bay

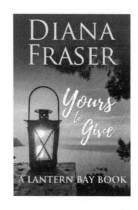

Yours to Give

Yours to Treasure

Yours to Cherish

Yours to Keep

Yours to Love

Yours Forever

Desert Kings

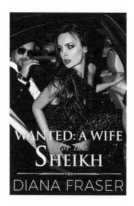

Wanted: A Wife for the Sheikh

The Sheikh's Bargain Bride

The Sheikh's Lost Lover

Awakened by the Sheikh

Claimed by the Sheikh

Wanted: A Baby by the Sheikh

The Sheikhs of Havilah

The Sheikh's Secret Baby

Bought by the Sheikh

The Sheikh's Forbidden Lover

Surrender to the Sheikh

Secrets of the Sheikhs

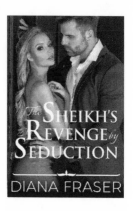

Italian Romance

Made in the USA
Middletown, DE
13 April 2022

64156710R00109